Austin extended his hand to help her up. "Sorry. Didn't mean to startle you."

"Totally my fault." Instead of taking his hand, she shoved herself to her feet.

He couldn't help how his gaze shifted to her wet T-shirt, which was plastered to her breasts.

Ella lifted her hands, palms out. "Didn't want to get you muddy." She nodded toward the spigot. "Sorry I used so much water, but I felt like a turkey roasting at Thanksgiving."

"Don't give yourself heatstroke."

She waved away his concern. "Nothing a shower, a load of laundry and the biggest Coke I can find won't cure."

Don't think of her in the shower. Don't think of her in the shower.

"I'll be back in the morning, and I'll bring you that ladder," she said.

"Okay." Did his voice sound as dry as his throat felt?

Thankfully, Ella slid into her truck and quickly shut the door, hiding the way her wet shorts were cupping her hips. As she drove away, he let out a slow breath,

turned on the spigot and stuck his own head under
the cool flow of water.

HOME ON THE RANCH

BY
TRISH MILBURN

First Published in Great Britain 2016
By Mills & Boon, an imprint of HarperCollins*Publishers*
1 London Bridge Street, London, SE1 9GF

© 2016 Trish Milburn

ISBN: 978-0-263-91972-1

23-0316

Our policy is to use papers that are natural, renewable and recyclable products and made from wood grown in sustainable forests.The logging and manufacturing processes conform to the legal environmental regulations of the country of origin.

Printed and bo
by CPI, Barce

Trish Milburn writes contemporary romance for the Mills & Boon Cherish line and paranormal romance for the Mills & Boon Nocturne series. She's a two-time Golden Heart® Award winner, a fan of walks in the woods and road trips, and a big geek girl, including being a dedicated Whovian and Browncoat. And from her earliest memories, she's been a fan of Westerns, be they historical or contemporary. There's nothing quite like a cowboy hero.

Thanks to MJ Fredrick,
for introducing me to Junk Gypsies.

To Amie and Jolie Sikes,
for being the Junk Gypsies and
inspiring the character of Ella Garcia.

Chapter One

He couldn't do it. As Austin Bryant stared at the front of the older house where he'd grown up, his breathing grew tight. It was as if what lay beyond the front door was already suffocating him as it had threatened to do during his childhood.

Somewhere in the distance, he heard the sound of an engine. The early May sun baked him like it could only in Texas, albeit not with the urban type of heat that came from that same sun beating down on metal and concrete. Even though sweat trickled from his neck toward the middle of his back, his feet refused to move.

He took a deliberate deep breath. It didn't matter how long he stood in the front yard of his grandparents' house, the monumental task he faced wasn't going to magically disappear. With his grandfather's passing, the time that he'd dreaded for years had come—cleaning out the house so he could sell it.

Austin inhaled another breath that felt as if it might scorch his lungs before he headed toward the front steps. He paused with the key in his hand, wondering if he could just walk away, sell the place as it was, let someone else deal with the cleaning and repairs.

But that didn't feel right. Despite everything, this had been his home when he was young. His earliest memories and dreams were formed here. No matter how hard it was, this was his task and his alone.

He shook his head, telling himself to just get on with things. The sooner he started, the sooner he could put it all behind him and stop thinking about what might have been.

The doorknob squeaked as he turned it, already making itself an item on his to-do list. He stepped across the threshold and into his past, the one he'd fled when he'd gone away to college. All around him, piled to the ceiling, was...stuff. Old magazines sat side by side with clothing that hadn't been worn in decades. Shelves of ceramic dust-catchers—cats, cowboy boots, ladies in frilly dresses, bells and God only knew what else—competed for space with chairs draped in more quilts and afghans than anyone in Texas should own.

He forced himself to take a few more steps into the house, but the farther he went the more he felt as if the piles of belongings were going to topple over and bury him alive. He'd had that particular nightmare for years, still did on occasion, and his lungs constricted just thinking about it. He spun in a slow circle, so overwhelmed he had no idea where to start. The task of getting rid of years of his grandparents' hoarding felt like he was facing scooping away Mount Everest with a teaspoon.

His grandparents had never been able to satisfactorily explain why they found it impossible to throw away any of their possessions. Not even when they'd passed the point of being able to know what items resided at the bottom of the piles. The one saving grace was that they hadn't been the type of hoarders who kept true garbage that attracted rodents or had dozens of cats. Still, it felt as if it was going to take the rest of his life to sort out what they'd left behind. Everything around him seemed to close in on him.

Not ready to face the rest, he turned and hurried back outside. The moment he stepped into the fresh air, the world expanded in size from what it had been only moments before, as if his lungs had received a sudden infusion of oxygen. Out here he was able to remember the good times, how his younger self had wanted so desperately to follow in his grandfather's footsteps here on this ranch. But the oppressive reality of the hoarding had been too much for Austin to handle, had robbed him of his chance to follow that particular dream.

Current reality hit him square in the chest, knocking thoughts of the past to the back of his brain where they belonged. He needed help, someone to haul all this stuff away. Because there was no way he was going to wade through everything. He didn't have the time or the inclination.

His stomach growled, reminding him that he hadn't eaten all day, not since the half sandwich after the funeral the day before. Needing food and distance, he stalked to his car and fled the ranch as if a wildfire were taking up the entirety of his rearview mirror. By the time he rolled into the city limits of Blue Falls, he felt like a fool. He was a grown man. A house full of junk shouldn't make him damn near hyperventilate.

He parked outside the Primrose Café and headed inside for lunch. Once his stomach was full, he'd make an actual plan that would get him back to Dallas before he was a decade older.

Before he even made it to a table, three people stopped him to express their sympathy over his grandfather's passing. That was both the blessing and the curse of a small town—no matter how long you'd been gone, people still remembered you.

After he seated himself and placed his order, he looked up to see Nathan Teague walking toward him, a to-go cup of coffee in hand.

"Hey, Austin." Nathan extended his hand for a shake, which Austin accepted. "Sorry to hear about your grandpa. He was a good man."

"Yeah, he was." Just because Austin had gotten out of his grandparents' house as soon as he could didn't mean he hadn't loved them. You could love people and still not understand them, still be at odds.

"How long you in town for?"

"Not sure. Need to get the place ready to sell. I'm actually in need of someone to haul off a bunch of junk. Who does that around here these days?"

"I'd suggest Ella Garcia." This answer didn't come from Nathan.

It took Austin a moment to recognize the older woman at the next table, but then he realized it was Verona Charles, the aunt of Elissa Mason, who'd gone to high school with him. "Pardon?"

Verona consulted her phone, then wrote something on a napkin and handed it to him. "Call Ella. She'll be able to help you out." With a smile, Verona stood and headed toward the front to pay her bill.

"You ever need to know something in Blue Falls, don't bother with the phone directory or the paper.

Just ask Verona," Nathan said. "Sorry to run, but I've got to go pick up my son for a doctor's appointment. Little booger broke his arm and it's cast removal day."

Austin said goodbye and was left with his just-arrived burger and fries and a napkin with a phone number. It seemed somewhat odd that a woman was running a trash removal business, but he didn't care if it was a band of little green Martians on the other end of the line as long as they could make quick work of his mounds of garbage.

Not wanting to waste even one moment, he stuck a fry in his mouth and dialed the number.

ELLA GARCIA STRAIGHTENED from where she'd been bent over her latest creative project and took a deep breath. Not that it was particularly refreshing since the temperature was nearing triple digits. She pulled a bandanna from the pocket of her cargo shorts and wiped the sweat off her forehead for what had to be the hundredth time. She walked over to the edge of her back porch and adjusted the fan she'd placed there to point toward where she was working in the backyard.

Satisfied with the angle of the mechanical breeze, she resumed sanding the rust off an antique tractor wheel that was going to become the main piece of a coffee table for one of her customers. As she scrubbed at a particularly difficult spot, her phone rang. She tossed her sandpaper onto the top of the upturned cable spool she was using as a workbench and pulled the phone from her back pocket. She didn't recognize the number, so she answered with her professional greeting.

"Restoration Decoration, this is Ella."

There was a pause on the other end of the line, causing her to think it might be a telemarketer. But then a man said, "Um, I'm calling for Ella Garcia."

"Speaking." He sure sounded tentative for a telemarketer. Man, that had to be one of the top five suckiest jobs in the world.

"I was given your number," he said, as if he'd suddenly remembered he should say something. "I need some junk hauled off."

"How much and what type?"

"A lot and you name it."

Excitement sparked to life inside Ella, her imagination dancing with her innate ability to turn one person's trash into another's treasure. She looked at the tractor wheel, mentally calculating how much work she had left to do in order to deliver the table by the deadline. She could always catch up on sleep after the buyer picked up the table, right? If she wanted to really grow her home decor business, she couldn't pass up the opportunity to acquire some raw materials on the cheap. She could spare a few hours.

"Okay, I'll come take a look. Can I get your name and address?"

"Austin Bryant, 345 Tumbleweed Road."

The combination of name and address made her realize he must be a relative of Dale Bryant's. A chill skated down her spine. This wouldn't be the first time she'd gotten materials that became available after someone's death, but never before had she been a witness to the person's passing.

"Okay, I can meet you there in an hour if that works for you."

"Sounds good."

On the drive to the Bryant ranch, Ella fought a queasy stomach as she tried to figure out how she'd greet Austin Bryant. Should she express her sympathy at Dale Bryant's passing? She didn't even know how Austin was related to him. Or would it be better to ignore the topic altogether?

As she drove through Blue Falls, she glanced at the hardware store, wondering if she'd ever be able to look at it the same again. She'd just parked on Main Street the week before, headed to the hardware store for a fresh supply of screws and sandpaper, when she'd seen the crowd surrounding someone lying on the sidewalk right outside the store's front door. She'd still been standing with the rest of the bystanders when the paramedics couldn't find a pulse and loaded Mr. Bryant into the ambulance. News traveled fast in a town the size of Blue Falls, so it hadn't been long before she'd heard they hadn't been able to save him.

But that wasn't the kind of story you shared with a grieving relative, especially when you'd never met him before. Trusting that she'd figure out the right thing to say when the time came, she turned off Main and headed out Tumbleweed Road.

A few minutes outside town, she started watching the numbers on mailboxes. She knew approximately where the ranch was, but she wasn't certain where the driveway sat. As she navigated a slight curve, she caught sight of the correct mailbox. The 5 at the end of the address had slipped and was hanging at an angle. Ella turned left onto the dirt and pea gravel drive that led out through scrub vegetation and a few cacti, then a line of live oak trees, their sprawling branches reminding her of octopuses.

After about half a mile, the vegetation gave way to an open area with an older house, barn, scattered outbuildings and rolling pastureland beyond. The spot felt cozy, cut off from the hustle and bustle of the rest of the world. Not that Blue Falls was a metropolis, but what she could see of the Bryant ranch seemed homey and probably filled with family history, even if perhaps it needed a little cosmetic TLC. Mr. Bryant had been in his seventies, a widower and not in good health. So it wasn't surprising that the place looked a little run-down.

She parked next to a shiny black sedan that looked out of place in the rural setting. As she slipped from the driver's seat, she spotted someone approaching from the house. Ella rounded the front of the truck but dang near tripped over her own feet when she looked up and saw the guy she assumed was Austin. In one glance, she noted his almond brown hair, striking blue eyes and a chiseled jaw that would be right at home on a cowboy in an old Western. She'd bet a considerable stack of cash that if she wiped the edges of her mouth, she'd find spontaneous drool.

"Miss Garcia?"

She continued to stare until her mind smacked the inside of her skull and said, *Say something, you goob!*

"Uh, yes." She extended her hand and he shook hers once before pulling back. It was over so quickly that she wanted to whimper. She'd gotten the fleeting notion that his hand was strong and warm. "I'm sorry about Mr. Bryant's passing. You're a relative?"

"He was my grandfather." He motioned for her to follow him toward the house.

Okay, so not a small talk kind of guy. Of course,

his mind was probably still occupied by grief at the loss of his grandfather. As she followed him, she had to force herself not to admire the breadth of his shoulders beneath his gray T-shirt.

Austin paused on the porch and shifted his beautiful blue gaze back to her. "I don't know if you know this, but my grandparents were hoarders. When I said there was a lot of junk, it wasn't an exaggeration."

Hoarders? Eek, what had she walked into? She had visions of mile-high refuse and a stench that would fell a skunk.

But when she followed him inside, she wasn't knocked over by the odor. It was a bit musty with a layer of that old-people smell they couldn't help, but considering how much stuff was just in the living room her nose was getting off easy.

She scanned the room, already picking out a few items that could be repurposed into eye-catching modern decor. So many people looked at a dated item and thought it had outlived its usefulness. She laid eyes on something such as the old cabinet-style TV and saw the cute shelving unit it could become with a little time, effort and paint.

"You can walk through the house if you like," Austin said. "But if you already know you're not interested, I understand."

She looked at him and would swear he'd stiffened up. The tension was radiating off him like heat rising off a long stretch of Texas highway in July. He did not want to be here. Whether it was because of memories or the monumental task of cleaning out his grandparents' things, she couldn't tell.

"I'll look around." As she walked from the living area into the kitchen, she tried not to let her excitement start galloping like a runaway horse. But it was difficult considering the wealth of tins, crockery, utensils and even an old percolator-style coffeepot on the stove.

As she moved from one room to another, Austin didn't leave the living room. It was as if he didn't want to be out of view of the front door. She didn't dawdle, but she took enough time to get some idea of what was available before returning to where Austin waited, definitely closer to the open door than when she'd left him.

"So how much to haul this away and how long will it take?" he asked.

Her gaze landed on several mason jars full of buttons behind him but she forced herself to focus on Austin, even if he did make her heart beat faster than normal.

"How much are you keeping?" she asked.

"None of it." He glanced around as the space between his dark eyebrows scrunched, as if he were perplexed why she would ask that question.

He wasn't the only one with questions. Had he already retrieved any mementos or heirlooms he wanted to keep? Or did he truly not want anything? She had never encountered a haul this large, and she worried about how she would manage to get it all out in a timely fashion and still meet her other obligations. But she'd have to because she was standing in the midst of a treasure trove of possible income.

Considering the situation, she reined in her giddiness. "I'll haul it away for free, but it'll take me several days since I'm a one-woman operation."

Austin's confusion deepened as he shifted his attention back to her. Damn, that man's eyes were enough to turn a woman's insides to puddles of undiluted desire.

"How can you make a living hauling trash for free?"

"It's not trash." She gestured to their surroundings. "I can make a lot of really wonderful home decor items from all this. Upcycling and repurposing are very popular right now, and a good way to keep items that still have use from ending up in landfills."

He shook his head. "If you say so. I just want it gone as quickly as possible."

She couldn't imagine throwing away a legacy as he seemed determined to do. She'd moved around so often as a kid that her belongings had necessarily been kept to a minimum. The only things she had left of her father were a quilt she'd made from his shirts and a small album of photos. Her mom, in grief at his loss, had given everything else away, as if doing so would ease her pain.

Was that what Austin was doing?

"Would you like me to start today?"

"If you can. But you might want to see the rest of it before you start."

"The rest?"

He motioned for her to follow him outside. This time, not only did she have to avert her eyes from his shoulders but also how nice his long legs looked in his jeans. Honestly, why couldn't it have been a frumpy niece who'd called her out here?

Austin headed toward the barn, not slowing his stride to accommodate her shorter legs. This dude was in a hurry, and she wondered if he would give

her enough time to go through his grandparents'
belongings. Would she have to haul it all away and
sift through it later? As she walked, she tried calculating the number of trips that would take, how many
hours of work.

When Austin opened the barn door, her prelimi-
nary calculations got blasted to smithereens.

He must have seen the surprised look on her face.
"I told you it was a lot."

"You weren't kidding."

"And there's more in the two small outbuildings
out back."

Holy macaroni. She strode into the barn, glancing
from side to side. Though it wasn't as packed as the
house, there was indeed a lot of extra stuff lining the
alleyway down the middle of the barn and occupy-
ing the stalls that didn't hold the one chestnut-colored
horse in residence.

"So people really buy stuff made from junk?"

The way he said "junk" rubbed her the wrong way,
as if what she put her heart and soul into was fool-
ish and the people who bought it even more so. But
she held her tongue. She wasn't going to let momen-
tary annoyance prevent her from scoring enough raw
materials to keep her hands and imagination busy for
months. And with plans in the works for a new arts
and crafts trail to lead tourists to the shops of local
artisans, this stockpile would help her have plenty of
offerings for new customers.

"Yes, and I appreciate the opportunity you've given
me here."

Austin crossed his arms across his chest, causing
her to gulp. Good grief, she hoped that hadn't been au-

dible. But really, she couldn't be blamed if it had been. Or for the fact she wondered what it would feel like to be wrapped in those well-defined arms. It wasn't her fault that the mere sight of him made her hormones jump up and start dancing the jitterbug.

"This is too much for one person to clear out," he said. "I should call in some more help."

"No, I can do it." It was going to be exhausting, but she hated the idea of a sanitation crew hauling everything off to the dump.

Austin let out a long exhale. "You have until I finish up some repairs and get the ranch listed. If it's not all gone by then, I'm calling in someone who can get everything out of here in a day."

She hastily agreed to his terms, even though she had no idea how she was going to manage such an undertaking on her own. Especially when she couldn't afford to hire any help.

"I'll get started now."

He gave her what felt like a long look with those gorgeous eyes then nodded once before walking past her out of the barn.

Unable to help herself, she turned and watched him stride away. Fearing he would sense her gaze, she spun back toward the interior of the barn. She'd set herself a near impossible task. She certainly didn't have time to ogle Austin Bryant, however pleasurable that might be.

Chapter Two

Austin battled the frustration eating at him from the inside as he walked back toward the house. For some reason that escaped him, he'd just agreed to let a woman who barely came up to the midway point on his chest have the time to haul all his grandparents' belongings away by herself. When she'd said that the piles of stuff could be useful, he'd been jerked back to his childhood, to when his grandmother had explained they couldn't throw anything out because they might need it someday.

Most of the time he couldn't remember what her voice sounded like, but he could hear her say that clear as day in his memory.

Even as a little boy, he'd known that there was no use for a black-and-white television that no longer worked or dozens of plastic butter containers that had been washed after the butter was eaten then stashed in the kitchen cabinets. What Ella Garcia saw in a lifetime of hoarding, he had no idea. And he didn't care as long as she got it out of his sight.

He fought against the urge to haul everything outside and set it on fire. But his rational brain managed to beat down that visceral need. While he might want it all gone now, realistically what did a few more days matter? It wasn't as if he didn't have enough work around the place to keep him busy while Ella toted away everything.

He stopped at the corner of the house and took a couple of deep breaths, ashamed that he let being here upset him so much. He needed to focus on things other than the past—things like fixing the sagging gutters on the house, checking the fencing around the ranch to see if it needed repairs, doing research to figure out what asking price he should shoot for when he talked to a real estate agent.

Movement out of the corner of his eye drew his attention. Ella Garcia hurried up the front steps of his grandparents' house. Now that he had a plan for clearing out the house and surrounding buildings, it was as if a layer of distraction that had been blinding him to her physical appearance had been peeled away.

Damn if he didn't feel his blood rush a little bit faster in his veins as he watched her fit legs carry her up the steps and toward the front door. As if they had a mind of their own, his eyes made a quick perusal up her legs and over her backside, all the way up to where she'd pulled her dark, curly hair into a pseudo ponytail on the back of her head. And his very male eyes liked what they saw, sending a message south to react accordingly.

Austin cursed under his breath. He already had about a dozen helpings too much on his plate. The last thing he needed was to be attracted to Ella. In a few days, his time in Blue Falls would be up and he'd be back in Dallas, where he wouldn't feel as if the world was caving in on him.

Needing to fill his mind with anything other than Ella Garcia's curves, he retraced his steps to the barn. While he didn't want to walk inside, he needed a ladder if he was going to start work on the gutters. At least the barn wasn't as bad as the house, he told himself as he stepped into the dim interior.

Luck was finally on his side when he spotted a ladder hanging on the wall about halfway down the alleyway. He started in that direction but paused when he reached Duke, his grandfather's sorrel stock horse.

"Hey, fella," he said as he scratched between Duke's ears. He smiled when he thought about how the horse had gotten his name, after John Wayne.

Austin's grandfather must have seen each of Wayne's movies at least a hundred times. The old VCR tapes were likely buried under fifty pounds of other stuff inside the house. Despite the happy memory of watching those movies with his grandfather, he didn't want the tapes. But he did sometimes find himself flipping channels at home or on a business trip and stopping to watch *The Searchers* or *The Man Who Shot Liberty Valance*.

His heart squeezed at the fact that he'd never again be able to talk to his grandfather, the man who'd been so much more than a grandparent to him. Dale Bryant had been the only father he'd ever known.

As if Duke could read Austin's thoughts, he lifted his head and bumped it against Austin's hand.

"You miss him, too, don't you?"

Duke let out a sad-sounding snort as if to give an affirmative answer.

Austin rubbed his hand along Duke's neck. "We'll go out for a ride tomorrow, boy." He let his hand drop away and made his way down the narrow path between wooden crates and old ranch equipment to reach the ladder.

But when he reached it, the crumbling wooden rungs made it obvious that he wasn't going to be using it to clean and fix the gutters. "Damn it."

"Something wrong?"

He spun toward the entrance to see Ella's petite form backlit by the strong sunlight outside.

"Useless ladder." He pointed toward where it hung on an old metal hook.

"I have one you can borrow. No need to get another if you're not keeping the place."

His instinct was to decline. Though when he stopped to think about it, that didn't make sense. What did make sense was not buying a ladder that he'd be using for only a few days, one that he couldn't transport in his car anyway.

"Thank you. I appreciate that."

"No problem." She held up something. "I found this and a bunch of other toys. I thought maybe they were yours when you were a kid and, well, you might want to keep them?"

It took him a moment to figure out that she was holding the engine to the wooden train set he'd had as a young boy. He hadn't even seen that in probably twenty years. For a split second, he thought maybe... He shook his head. "No. Like I said, there's nothing here I want. If you find things you can't use, I'm happy to pay you to haul them away. Or leave them and I'll have a trash crew come in and get the rest."

She glanced at the toy in her hand, and he'd swear he saw a flicker of sadness in her expression. Maybe she was just one of those people who got attached to things. He wasn't. Things had to be useful, a means to an end. There was no other reason to have them.

And yet there was some strange part of him that wanted to keep the train engine simply because she evidently wanted him to for some reason. Crazy.

"Okay," Ella finally said. "I'll bring the ladder with me tomorrow unless you need it sooner. I could take a small load of stuff home then come back with it."

"No, that's not necessary. There are plenty of other things I can do without it." And he'd rather she make a fast dent in the piles before they decided to multiply when he had his back turned.

She gave a quick nod then headed out of the barn.

He sighed and realized the only thing that was going to give him any sort of relief from his frustration was a ride out across the ranch. He knew that from years of experience.

Well, that's not all that could give you relief.

Jeez, the woman had been on his property only half an hour at most and he was already having sexual thoughts about her.

You're only human. A man.

Yeah, but he wasn't an animal. And Ella Garcia was definitely not the type of woman for him. Her excitement over getting to possess piles of junk, as if she'd won the kid lottery on Christmas morning, told him that much.

Needing a lot of fresh air and wide-open sky, preferably far away from the temptation of the woman currently carrying a big box out to her truck, he moved toward the tack room. Once he retrieved his grandfather's saddle, he walked over to Duke's stall. "Change of plans, boy."

Maybe somewhere out on his grandparents' acreage he'd find a sense of calm and his common sense.

ELLA SHOVED A box of vintage lace doilies into the back of her truck, already imagining the beautiful lampshades she could make from them. As she raised her hand to wipe sweat from her forehead for what had to be the thousandth time since she'd arrived at the Bryant ranch, the muscles in her arms screamed at her. She was sweaty, dirty, aching and needed a Coke approximately the size of the Blue Falls water tower, but she was going to cram as much stuff into her truck as possible. The quicker she emptied the house, the better. She didn't want to risk Austin changing his mind, thinking it was taking her too long. It would be a crime for all these items to end up at the dump.

She just wished she could clone herself a couple of times to make the work go faster. So would having Austin's help, but then that's what he'd "hired" her for, right? Plus, he'd disappeared on his grandfather's horse a few hours ago. The moment she'd seen him astride the horse, riding off across the pasture, she'd nearly tripped over her feet again. That certainly was a dangerous and annoying effect for a guy to have on a girl. If she wasn't careful, she was going to face-plant in the driveway and not be able to tell him why. She'd have to claim supreme klutziness or something.

If she'd thought he looked like a movie star cowboy earlier, him astride a horse with the wide, blue sky as a backdrop had only increased that impression tenfold. If he'd been wearing a cowboy hat and boots, it was possible she would have just drooled herself into dehydration.

Despite the lack of traditional cowboy attire, there had been something so totally right about the sight of him astride that horse, like he belonged here in this place.

Why she thought that, she had no idea. After all, she didn't have a lot of experience with deep connections to a place. Growing up in a military family came with a certain rootlessness. Only since moving to Blue Falls had she started to feel a real connection to a slice of the world. According to the friends she'd made here, it was one of those small towns where people enjoyed growing up and many liked to stay.

Except, evidently, Austin Bryant. When he'd shown her around the place and asked about how long it would take her to empty all the buildings, he'd been fighting a barely contained fidgetiness. It was as if he thought the place was going to cause him to break out in a rash if he stayed too long. And though Dale Bryant had been a nice guy, it seemed his grandson couldn't be rid of anything that reminded him of his grandparents fast enough.

With another swipe at the sweat beading on her forehead, she headed back into the house.

By the time she was wedging the last possible thing—an old sewing box filled with lots of notions—into her truck, she was so tired and hot that if there were a flowing creek nearby she'd just lie down in it, clothes and all.

As if the universe were offering her the next best thing, she spotted a water spigot between the house and the barn. Like a desert traveler heading toward a mirage, she crossed to the spigot and turned it on. She stuck her entire head underneath the flow of water, and it felt so good that she had to resist the urge to stay underneath it until she ran the water source dry.

She did extend the top half of her body under the flow, soaking her T-shirt and bra. Good thing she was heading straight home because she no doubt looked like she'd been dragged behind a boat across Blue Falls Lake. When she got her truck unloaded, she was going to take the longest shower in the history of showers.

Though she didn't want to, she turned off the spigot and wiped the water from her face as she stood. She opened her eyes to find a man standing a few feet away. An involuntary scream left her mouth before recognition hit. This time, she wasn't able to prevent the tangled-feet phenomenon from dumping her flat on her butt in the mud she'd just created.

WHEN AUSTIN HAD headed out to ride the fence line earlier, he'd left behind a woman carrying away his grandparents' things. As he stared down at Ella now, she looked more like she'd fallen in a stock tank filled with water.

He extended his hand to help her up. "Sorry. Didn't mean to startle you."

She made a dismissive gesture with a muddy hand. "Totally my fault." Instead of taking his hand, she shoved herself to her feet.

He couldn't help how his gaze shifted to her wet T-shirt, which was plastered to her perfectly rounded breasts. He barely managed to lift his eyes toward her face in time to prevent her from noticing his blatant staring.

Ella lifted her hands, palms out. "Didn't want to get you muddy." She nodded toward the spigot. "Sorry I used so much water, but I felt like a turkey roasting at Thanksgiving."

"Don't give yourself heatstroke." He certainly didn't need her passing out in the driveway, burying herself under mounds of clothing or magazines that hadn't seen the light of day since the '90s or before.

She waved away his concern. "Nothing a shower, a load of laundry and the biggest Coke I can find won't cure."

Don't think of her in the shower. Don't think of her in the shower.

He forced himself to look at her truck instead of her. "I can't believe you got so much stuff in one load." Not that it would likely look like much had been removed from the mountains the house contained.

"I'm a master at packing lots into a small space."

His skin itched at the very idea. Were the boxes and bags and miscellaneous items simply relocating to take up residence for years more in some other space too small to adequately contain them?

Not his problem.

"I'll be back in the morning, and I'll bring you that ladder," she said.

He glanced back at Ella to see her already moving toward the driver's side of her truck.

"Okay." Did his voice sound as dry as his throat felt?

When she opened the door on the truck, she pulled a plastic bag from behind the seat and placed it where she could sit her muddy bottom on it.

Thankfully, she slid into the truck and quickly shut the door, hiding the way her wet shorts were also cupping her hips. She started the engine then tossed him a wave before she headed down the driveway. He was reminded of the Clampett family's truck on old reruns of *The Beverly Hillbillies*, piled high with all their possessions as they headed to California after striking it rich.

Only Ella Garcia hadn't struck it rich, even if she sort of acted as though she had.

As she disappeared beyond the trees, he let out a slow breath, turned on the spigot and stuck his own head under the cool flow of water.

Chapter Three

Ella moaned as her alarm clock belted out beeps the next morning. "You've got to be kidding me," she mumbled into her pillow. Hadn't she fallen asleep about ninety seconds ago?

Honestly, if she had a baseball bat handy, the clock's remaining seconds would be numbered in single digits.

Since mind control sadly didn't work on the alarm, she rolled over and slapped it off. She stared up at the ceiling with every muscle in her body staging a coup. But today wasn't going to be any easier. In fact, instead of a partial day of clearing out the Bryant house, she was going to be at it all day for multiple loads. Not for the first time she allowed herself to fantasize about her business growing so much that she could afford an employee or two to help out with the pickups, deliveries, all the miscellaneous stuff that ate into her design time.

But fantasizing about it wasn't going to make it come true. Getting her tired butt out of bed just might. Eventually.

After a few minutes in the bathroom, she dressed and headed out to load the ladder in the truck. Once it was secured, she headed toward town. More specifically, the Mehlerhaus Bakery.

Keri Teague, the owner, looked up when Ella walked into the bakery. If heaven smelled any better than this place…well, Ella wasn't sure that was possible.

"You look as if you could use some coffee."

"You, my friend, are correct. And one of those cinnamon rolls that's as big as my head."

Keri slid the door on the back of the glass display case open and reached for one of the cinnamon rolls that was, no lie, the size of a salad plate.

"Actually, make it two rolls and two large coffees."

"You really in need of sugar and caffeine or you buying some for Austin Bryant, too?"

"Can't hurt to come bearing breakfast when I'm hoping to have time to get everything he's offered."

Keri lifted a brow. "And just what exactly has he offered?"

"Fine, twist the tired lady's words."

Keri laughed as she bagged up the rolls. "I haven't seen Austin in a long time, but as I remember he wasn't exactly hard to look at."

"I'm too busy looking at all the raw materials I'm hauling out of his grandparents' house."

"Uh-huh." Keri gave her a look that said she didn't buy one word of what Ella had just said.

"Okay, fine. The guy is good-looking. He also couldn't be more anxious to get the hell out of here and back to wherever he came from."

"Dallas. He's got some big job at an energy company, I think."

Well, that explained the nice car. What it didn't explain was how at home he looked on that horse, riding out toward a herd of cattle. Of course, that could just be remnants of his childhood still lingering.

Keri placed a couple of to-go coffees on the counter beside the cinnamon rolls. "Oh, and by the way, you might want to know that the person who pointed Austin in your direction was Verona."

Oh, great. So far Ella had managed to not become the town matchmaker's target, but she'd guessed it was only a matter of time.

"That woman has entirely too much time on her hands," Ella said as she passed over the money for her breakfast. "Plus, I think there ought to be a rule that you should have to be a native of Blue Falls to be targeted by her."

"No, no. You live here, you take the same chances as every other unattached person."

"You're just saying that because you're happily married and don't have to worry about it anymore."

"Well, there is that."

Ella laughed and grabbed her purchases. "At least I won't have to worry about it long. I'm guessing Austin Bryant heads home before the week is over."

"Oh, that's plenty of time for Verona to work her magic. Plus, even if he leaves, she'll just try to find you someone else."

Ella stuck out her tongue at Keri before heading toward the door, which just made her friend laugh as if she hadn't had so much fun in ages.

As Ella headed toward her truck, she thought about what Keri had said and tried to figure out who Verona might try to pair her up with should Austin pull a Houdini out of town. She couldn't think of a single person who interested her.

Well, that wasn't entirely true. The fact that she'd bought an extra coffee and monster cinnamon roll proved that, didn't it?

She shook her head and made a sound of frustration at herself as she started the engine and headed off toward her long day of work. That's what she needed to focus her attention on, not the long, tall Texan she'd be seeing again in about fifteen minutes.

As she pulled onto the road that led back to the ranch, her nerves started that annoying dancing thing again. Jeez, it was as if she'd never seen a handsome guy before. Heck, there were plenty traipsing through Blue Falls on a daily basis, locals and cowboys in town for the regular rodeos. Why did this particular owner of a Y chromosome set her insides to doing funny, not normal things?

Yes, he was hot as a firecracker, but he was also sort of grumpy. Granted, that could be chalked up to grief and too much to do in too short a time, but still. It wasn't as if he was going to up and sweep her off her feet. Not that she wanted to be swept. Did she?

Crap, maybe she had suffered a heatstroke the day before.

When she pulled within view of the house, Austin's car wasn't there.

"Well, that was anticlimactic." She glanced at the bag with the two cinnamon rolls and at the extra coffee container riding in her cup holder. "More for me, I guess."

Not willing to go into the house even if it happened to be unlocked, she unloaded the ladder, leaning it

against the side of the house, then retrieved her breakfast. She hopped up on the lowered tailgate and dug
in. At the first bite, she closed her eyes and paid attention to nothing but the cinnamon and sugar tango-
ing across her tongue. No matter how many times she
ate something from Keri's bakery, she never ceased to
be amazed at the woman's magical ways with sweets.

Opening her eyes, she took a drink of coffee and
looked out beyond the barn to the field stretching
toward the horizon. It really was peaceful out here.
She liked her little rental house fine, but it didn't have
this kind of view. One couldn't call a highway and
the back side of Blue Falls' small industrial park particularly scenic.

The quiet of the morning gave way to the sound of
a car engine heading toward her. She almost choked
on the bite she'd just taken when she spotted Austin's car.

*Oh, get a grip. You're here to work, not ogle and
daydream.*

"You're here early," he said as he got out of the car.

"Lots to do." She lifted the white paper bag that
contained the second cinnamon roll in one hand and
the extra coffee in the other. "Breakfast?"

He gave her an odd look, as if he didn't quite understand her one-word question. "You brought me
food?"

"I was already at the bakery. Not hard to add an
extra cinnamon roll. Plus, I didn't know if you were
staying out here without the kitchen being stocked."

"I'm not staying on the ranch." He said it quickly,
with the same tone she could imagine him using if
she'd accused him of sleeping in a pigsty.

"Okey-dokey," she said.

Austin ran his hand back over his hair. The movement drew attention to his rather nice arm. She wondered what else was hiding underneath his navy blue T-shirt.

"Sorry," he said as he closed the distance between them. "Didn't mean to snap at you. Just got a lot on my mind." He peeked inside the paper bag and whistled.

"Yeah, it's big."

He glanced over to where she'd made her way through about half of hers. "You can eat that whole thing?"

"Every delectable bite." She smiled, and when he offered a bit of a smile back, she dang near melted and slid off the tailgate.

If that wasn't bad enough, when he took a bite of his cinnamon roll then licked at some of the icing at the edge of his mouth, she was pretty sure she spontaneously got pregnant.

Before she embarrassed herself so much she'd have to move out of Texas, she hopped down to the ground and wrapped up the rest of her cinnamon roll for later, when Austin Bryant wasn't standing in front of her making her want to take a bite out of him instead.

As she rounded the back of the truck to put the bag in the cab, she pointed toward the house. "You can now have fun cleaning the gutters."

Austin glanced toward where she'd propped the ladder and nodded. "Thanks. I think."

She laughed a little. "Not looking forward to it?"

"Have you ever known anyone who looked forward to cleaning gutters?"

"Excellent point."

Not knowing what else to say to keep their limited conversation going, she grabbed her tablet from the glove compartment and nodded toward the front porch. "Well, I better get busy, too."

As she walked toward the house, she thought how it was a good thing Verona Charles wasn't anywhere nearby. Because one look at Ella's face would be all the encouragement the older woman needed to go full-on matchmaker, no matter the fact that Austin was clearing out, not moving in.

She took another big swig of her coffee to fight off the fatigue brought on by too little sleep the night before. And, honestly, several nights before that. Tonight wasn't looking as if it was going to be any different. But sacrifices had to be made if she wanted to build her business, move into a bigger space where she could store her finds, have an area to spread out and work, and eventually have a storefront.

Not wanting to get any more behind on her inventory tracking than she already was thanks to the load from the day before, she set up her tablet on the kitchen table and started listing everything as she went through it. Logging everything before she carried it out to the truck slowed her down, but she knew from experience that if she allowed herself to get too behind she ended up overwhelmed. She probably didn't have the best tracking system in the world, but it worked for her.

She was in the midst of inputting a box of vintage sewing patterns, already imagining decoupaging them onto tables and chairs and old sewing machine cabinets, when the unholiest racket came from outside. Fearing Austin had fallen off the ladder, she jumped up and ran out the front door.

By the time she rounded the corner of the house, he was halfway down the ladder with his hand to his forehead. The gutter hung by only one end, the opposite end nearly scraping the ground as it swung like a pendulum on a grandfather clock. She spotted the telltale red of blood around the edge of Austin's fingers.

"It hit you in the head?"

"Yeah." He growled the response, sounding as if he'd love to add a few choice curses after his single-word answer.

"Here, let me see," she said, taking a few steps toward him.

"I'm fine."

"Don't be stubborn."

He glanced up at her, raising the eyebrow on the undamaged side of his face. "Little bossy, aren't you?"

She waved away his description. "Just practical. Now come on." She motioned for him to follow her, and was sort of surprised when he actually did.

But when she headed inside, he stopped halfway up the front steps. Not wanting his unwillingness to go inside to prevent her from tending his wound, she motioned for him to sit on the steps. "I'll be right back."

She made for the bathroom, which was cluttered but not as crammed full as the rest of the house. After locating a clean washcloth, some hydrogen peroxide and an assortment of other first-aid supplies, she hurried back outside to find Austin with his feet on the second step and lying back on the porch. For a moment, she thought maybe he'd passed out. But he turned his head toward her.

Ella plopped down next to him, sitting cross-legged, and set to work washing away the blood and cleaning the wound. As cuts went, it wasn't very big. But head lacerations were notorious for bleeding like crazy, making the injured party look like Carrie on prom night.

"I suppose I'll live?"

The rumble of Austin's voice so close sent delicious shivers across her skin. Why hadn't she noticed his voice was so sexy it made her want to hop out of her clothes?

Oh, good grief. All work and no play were making Ella a naughty-minded girl.

"You should be fine as long as you don't try head-butting any more gutters."

He sighed and tried to sit up. Not even thinking about her action, she pressed down on his shoulder.

"Hang on. Let the bleeding stop so I can get a bandage on it. When was the last time you had a tetanus shot?"

"No clue. Probably when I was in school."

"I'd suggest getting one."

"I'll be fine."

She sighed in exasperation. Now who was being stubborn? "Tell yourself that when you're spasming so hard you break your bones."

He looked like he might respond but then seemed to reconsider.

Ella tried not to think about how close her bare leg was to his bare arm as she leaned forward to apply antibiotic cream to the cut. She wasn't sure if heat was really coming off his body like he was a furnace, or if she was just flushing from the images traipsing through her mind. Things such as Austin back on that ladder but without a shirt and his jeans hanging low on his hips.

She made a frustrated sound without thinking about it.

"What's wrong?" Austin asked as she affixed the bandage.

"It's just blasted hot out here. I feel like I'm going to cook."

The way he was looking up at her certainly wasn't helping lower her temperature either.

"You do know you live in Texas, right?"

"Doesn't make it any less true."

For what felt like an unnaturally long moment, he stared up at her before finally lifting himself to a sitting position and propping his forearms on his legs, letting his hands dangle between his knees.

"Got to admit I'm not used to this anymore," he said. "Air-conditioning spoils a person."

"All that time sitting in an office?" She couldn't help being curious about this man who did zippy things to her lady parts.

He glanced over at her. "How do you know I work in an office?"

"Well, I didn't figure you were a highway worker after the AC comment." She paused. "And Keri at the bakery might have mentioned you worked at an energy company or something."

He huffed out a little laugh. "I manage to forget how everyone knows everything about everyone here."

"Trust me, it's not the only place that's like that."

"Where are you from originally?"

She made a circular motion in the air with her index finger. "All over. Army brat."

"Bet that was interesting."

She shrugged. "Yes and no. Japan was neat. I still love Japanese food."

"Not a lot of that in Blue Falls."

"No, but I like it here." She glanced out across the land where Austin had grown up. "I used to envy kids who got to stay in one place."

"We always want what we don't have."

"I guess that's true." Despite the fact she'd known this man all of a single day, she found herself wondering what Austin wanted that he didn't have. Other than to get his grandparents' property cleared out and sold, that was. "Well, if you need more first aid, just yell. I'm going back to work."

Before she could lift herself to her feet, Austin stood and held out his hand. As she looked at that proffered hand, some heretofore unknown alarm system in her head started clanging as though Blue Falls was about to be bombed by B-52s. Some instinct said if she touched his hand, she was going to have trouble sleeping at night, no matter how exhausted she was.

But then she couldn't really refuse without appearing rude. Telling herself to think about anything other than Austin—the price of bread, how many elements she could remember from the periodic table, how dandelions grew back so blasted fast—she accepted his hand. Dang if he didn't pull her up as easily as if she weighed no more than one of those dandelions. And as she feared, sizzles of electricity raced up her arm and proceeded through the rest of her body.

"Thanks," she said, wincing inwardly at how forced her cheery voice sounded.

Austin released her hand so suddenly it was as if her touch had turned scorching hot. Trying not to be offended, she gave him a quick smile and retreated inside. But when she returned to the area of the kitchen where she'd been logging her finds, she had a hard time focusing on the task. In fact, she found it hard to sit still. Darn her overactive imagination. It was having a field day up in her head, wondering what that large, warm hand would feel like touching her face, his fingers finding their way through her riot of curls to the back of her head.

No, she wouldn't think about his lips. Nope, nope, nope.

Determined to regain some of her suddenly AWOL sanity, she decided to tackle a closet in the master bedroom. But when she stepped through the doorway, her gaze landed on the bed covered with an old-fashioned chenille bedspread. She knew she was in trouble when instead of wondering what she could do with the chenille, she had a mental flash of crawling beneath it with a very hot and naked Austin Bryant.

Chapter Four

After Ella retreated into the house, Austin let out his breath and ran his fingers back through his hair. When was the last time a woman had taken care of him like Ella just had? His grandmother when he'd been a kid scraping knees and elbows around the ranch? It freaked him out how nice it had felt, her soft hands being gentle with his stupid injury but quick and efficient at the same time.

The moment her small fingers had touched his skin, a wave of heat had raced through him that had nothing to do with the climbing temperature outside.

Damn, of all the women toward whom he could have a powerful attraction.

With a shake of his head, he returned to the ladder and what he should be thinking about—working to get this ranch ready to sell.

But as he wrestled with the gutters, his mind kept wandering back to the woman inside the house. He seemed to always end up on dates with taller, leggy blondes. He'd assumed that was just his type. Even in high school, he'd dated Sophie Bellermine, who'd been a blonde and the center on the basketball team.

So why were his thoughts and hormones latching

on to a petite brunette whose curls seemed to be hosting a party on her head?

What was she doing in the house anyway? Yesterday, she'd been like a whirlwind, speeding back and forth to her truck. Today she seemed to disappear inside for longer stretches of time. He just hoped she didn't fall victim to an avalanche of his grandparents' myriad possessions.

No, not his grandparents' stuff, not anymore. Now it all belonged to him—at least until Ella could get it off the property.

As if thinking about her conjured her, Ella strode out to the truck carrying a box of...something. He didn't even care what it was. Just wanted it gone.

He paused in the midst of attaching another portion of the gutter that had pulled away from the roof to watch her. Her legs might not be as long as a supermodel's, but they certainly packed a lot of punch. Fit, smooth, tempting. His body stood at attention, making his jeans grow uncomfortable. But he couldn't stop watching.

He would have been better off if a burly, hairy guy had shown up to do the job, but if someone had to be here for several days, she was a damn sight nicer to look at.

When she turned to walk back to the house, she headed in his direction instead. She shaded her eyes as she looked up at him.

"Glad to see you haven't bled out."

No, his blood was too busy rushing to other parts of his body to mess with a measly head wound.

"Despite evidence to the contrary, I'm not normally accident-prone."

"Good to know, because I start charging for the second injury."

He laughed, surprising himself. It seemed to release some well of tension within him he hadn't truly been aware of. His arm and leg muscles relaxed, including the death grip he'd had on the rung of the ladder. He took a deep breath, maybe the first true one he'd taken since getting the call about his grandfather.

"You okay?" Ella asked.

"Yeah." He nodded once toward the house. "How's it going?"

"Good. I'm logging as I go so I can at least pretend I have a tracking system for supplies."

She was taking the time to log piles and piles and piles of stuff that he would have sworn had outlived its usefulness? "Won't that slow you down?"

He thought he saw a hint of a wince cross her face, but she was too far away to tell for sure.

"Some. I guessed that you still had quite a bit of work to do before you were ready to list the place."

"I do. But I can't do anything inside until it's cleared out."

Ella slipped her hands into the back pockets of her shorts, probably unaware of the way that movement accentuated her figure and threatened to make him topple off the ladder.

"How much more do you have to do outside?"

Plenty to keep him busy for several more days, but how could he convey that he just needed all the crap gone, out of his sight, out of his life without sounding like he had an irrational hatred for inanimate objects?

"A bit." *Way to be specific, dude.*

"Got it, pick up the pace."

Before he could respond, she spun and disappeared around the corner of the house. Frustrated by his mental hang-up about his grandparents' stash, he looked up at the cloudless sky and let out a long sigh. He needed to chill, let Ella do her thing. After all, her hauling everything away wasn't costing him a penny. He needed to appreciate that positive fact instead of letting his past make him want to throw however much it cost at someone to haul everything out of here today.

Calm the hell down.

Despite his "a bit" answer to her question, he had more than enough to keep him busy that didn't require him stepping foot in the house.

It seemed being away from Blue Falls for several years had made him forget how to cope with things out of his control—concentrating only on the thing directly in front of him and pretending everything else didn't exist. Movement out of the corner of his eye revealed itself to be Ella striding to the truck, her arms full of several small, teetering boxes.

How the heck was he supposed to pretend Ella Garcia didn't exist?

ELLA STALKED BACK into the house, frustration and fatigue gnawing at her. She wasn't really mad at Austin. After all, he'd been up-front with her about wanting the place cleared out as quickly as possible, and she'd agreed. But she dreaded trying to log everything after she'd shoved it...somewhere. She couldn't think now about the fact that she didn't have enough space for everything here, not even close. She'd have to figure that out later, when she had to move everything yet again to log it, then put it back wherever she'd crammed it. She didn't have time for doubling or tripling her efforts, but it wasn't as if she was willing to walk away from the current windfall either. Even if the faster she got away from Austin Bryant, the better.

When she'd been tending the cut on his forehead earlier, her fingers could have easily continued exploring if she hadn't forcefully reined them in. The man was too good-looking for her comfort. She kept having to dissuade herself from making up reasons to go out and talk to him just to hear the sexy rumble of his voice, to see how nicely his jeans fit his backside, to watch the play of the muscles in his arms as he worked.

It sure had been a while since infatuation had hit her this hard and this fast, not since she'd fallen instantly head over heels for Jacob O'Riley when she was a freshman in high school, only to have him and his family move to Ohio. She remembered crying herself to sleep the night she'd found out that he'd moved, convinced it was the end of the world.

Well, she wasn't going to be crying over Austin Bryant, and it wasn't going to be the end of the world when he went back to Dallas. Sure, she'd miss the whole sexy-package thing he had going on, but soon enough she'd be buried in her work and too darn busy to wonder about what Austin was doing more than two hundred miles away.

No, she'd enjoy the male scenery while they were here crossing paths, and that would be that.

Several times throughout the day, she came across items that she wanted to ask Austin if he'd like to keep. But he'd made it clear he wasn't interested, which saddened her. How many times had she wished she had more keepsakes, more tangible items with memories attached? But not everyone was like that. Still, something in her gut told her he wasn't as unattached as he claimed.

By the time she'd unearthed an old treadle sewing machine, her truck was filling up again. She stood back, eyeing the half of the bedroom where she'd been working for the past couple of hours. She'd made a good-size dent in the contents of the room and was now able to see one whole wall.

Ella looked out the window, estimating the space left in the truck versus the space needed for the sewing machine. After she had time to examine it more thoroughly, she'd figure out what to do with it. For now, it was destined for that rectangle of space left at the back of her truck bed. She hated to do it, but she was going to have to ask Austin for help with this one.

But when she went outside, he was nowhere to be found. She walked around the house, noting that the gutters appeared to all be in their proper spots, but no Austin. She spun in a circle, but she still didn't see him. Oh well, she wasn't going to chase him down, wherever he'd gone. It might take some wrestling and grunting, but somehow she'd get the sewing machine in the truck. After all, she was used to doing things by herself, a necessity of single life.

Then she'd go home, unload everything and faceplant in her bed until she had to get up and do it all over again. Maybe she'd be so tired by the time she crawled into bed that she wouldn't even have the energy to fantasize about Austin Bryant joining her there.

AUSTIN STOOD IN the tack room of the barn staring at little pieces of the life he'd enjoyed sharing with his grandfather. Unlike the rest of the indoor spaces on the ranch, this one small room was orderly and free of clutter. When he hadn't been outside, this had been the place where he'd felt able to breathe. Odd since the room was so small compared with everything around it.

He took the couple of steps that brought him within reach of the wooden pegs on the wall where more memories hung. He ran his hand down the rough fabric of his grandfather's old work jacket he'd used in the winter. How many times had Austin seen his grandfather wearing it as he'd gone out to take care of the cattle or to work on machinery?

Austin had never felt more alone than he did in that moment, when it really hit him that all of his family was gone. Oh, his dad might be out there somewhere, but he wouldn't know the man if they sat beside each other on a plane.

He grabbed the hat he'd come in here to retrieve and headed back out, wondering when the heavy sadness that seemed to have settled in his chest would dissipate.

When he stepped out into the sunlight, he noticed Ella at the bottom of the front steps, struggling to maneuver his grandmother's old sewing machine.

Damn fool woman was going to hurt herself. Then wouldn't they be a pair, unable to get through an entire day without sustaining an injury.

He put on his old hat and ran toward her. Without making a big deal about it, he lifted the heavier end of the machine that was still teetering on the steps and helped her carry it to the truck. Ella did her best to hide how hard it was for her to carry the weight on her end, and he admired her for it. Sure, it could be seen as stubborn, but he liked the fact that she worked hard and did things on her own. Sure, any decent guy had the instinct to take care of a woman, but he couldn't stand the women who acted helpless to get a man's attention.

Whatever problems he'd had with the way his grandparents had chosen to live, he could never accuse them of being lazy. They had been the two most hardworking people he'd ever known. He did his best to follow in their footsteps in that regard, if not others.

When they reached the back of the truck, he pointed toward the bit of empty space left in the bed. "Hop up and I'll lift most of the weight up to you."

He doubted the wisdom of his direction when Ella's shorts stretched across her hips as she shoved herself up into the back of the truck. When he forced himself to avert his eyes, they landed on the top of the closed sewing machine. Out of nowhere, a memory of his grandmother sitting at the machine stitching together the top for a patchwork quilt assaulted him. He couldn't have been more than four or five at the time, but the image was as clear as if he'd watched the scene only yesterday.

"You okay?" Ella asked.

"Yeah. Just remembered a time I saw my grandmother working on this." He rubbed his hand across the wooden top. Had the quilt she'd been piecing in that memory been the one that ended up on his bed? That part he couldn't remember.

"So maybe you should keep it?"

For a moment, he even considered it. But only a moment. He shook his head. "I have no use for it, and I can't even remember the last time I saw it."

He looked up in time to see Ella press her lips together in a straight line, signaling she didn't understand him. He guessed that went both ways.

"Let's get this thing loaded." He took the brunt of the weight of the sewing machine as they lifted it up into the bed. And it was a good thing because he realized Ella looked on the verge of collapse. As soon as the machine was in the truck, she sank onto the side of the bed.

Had his assertion that he needed things cleared out fast pushed her to work too hard? Guilt twisted inside him, right alongside the hunger. He realized he hadn't eaten anything since the cinnamon roll, and he didn't think Ella had either. And it was already late afternoon.

"I think we need a break and some food," he said.

"I'm okay," she said with a faint wave of her hand that proved she wasn't. Not to mention the audible growl of her stomach that she seemed to be hoping he hadn't heard.

"Well, I'm not. I feel like I could eat half of one of those out there." He pointed toward a few head of his grandfather's herd huddled under one of the few trees that dotted the pasture.

The edges of her mouth turned up a bit in a tired smile. "Since you put it that way." She patted a pile of boxes next to where she sat. "Let me get this tied down and I'll get out of your hair."

"Leave it. Trust me, no one is going to make off

with it, and there's a zero percent chance it's going to rain."

The slight widening of her dark brown eyes told him she was just catching on that he meant for them to go eat together. He half couldn't believe it himself. But it wasn't a date, just him making sure she ate and drank enough on his watch. The last thing he needed was something to happen to her that would make his stay here even longer.

Sure, tell yourself all kinds of lies. You just want to sit across the table from her.

Okay, maybe that was true. He was a guy, and guys liked to look at pretty women. It was hardwired from day one. Plus, he really was hungry.

"What are you in the mood for?" she asked.

She really didn't want him to answer that question. Instead, he shrugged. "As long as it's food, not picky."

"Pizza?"

"Sounds good."

She nodded once and got to her feet. Before he could think better of it, he grabbed her at the waist and lifted her to the ground. When she broke contact and took a step back, Ella looked every bit as startled by his action as he was.

"Um, thanks." She didn't quite meet his eyes.

"No problem." Oh, except for how all the nerves in his body had jumped to full attention the moment he'd placed his hands at her small waist. "Don't want you taking a header into the dirt. One head wound per day is the rule around here."

She smiled, easing the tension he'd caused. "Hope you're buying, because I plan to put away a boatload of pizza."

"It's the least I can do for your medical services and how hard you're working to clear everything out around here."

"I should wait until after you've paid for the pizza to say this, but you're doing me a huge favor, letting me take all this stuff. I'll put it to good use."

He couldn't imagine how, but if it made her happy and it made him happy, he wasn't going to argue with a win-win situation.

As he drove toward town, Ella visibly relaxed in the passenger seat and pointed both air vents on her side of the car at her face.

"This feels heavenly," she said. "My plan is to take something I get from your place and make enough profit to fix the stupid AC in my truck."

"It doesn't work?"

"Pooped out on me a few weeks ago. I'm running the two-sixty air now—two windows at sixty miles per hour." She laughed a little at her own bit of humor.

She might be making light of the situation, but no AC in Texas was like no water in the desert—unbearable. Working outside in the heat was one thing, but living without it when you were in your house or car was just cruel and unusual punishment.

He slowed down when they came up behind the mail carrier, then pulled around via the opposite lane. Ella waved at the woman driving the little red pickup.

"So you're not from here," he said. "How did you end up in Blue Falls?"

"I visited with a friend and liked it so much I made it a goal to move here. It just sort of fit my personality."

He glanced over at her. "How so?"

"It's friendly, eclectic, has small-town charm but isn't so insular that newcomers are treated like invaders. It just seemed to be a nice place for people who've lived here their entire lives to share space with people who choose to relocate here."

"Never thought of it that way."

"Probably not at the front of your mind when you live so far away," she said as she readjusted one of her air vents. "How'd you end up in Dallas anyway?"

"It's where I got a job after college."

"So Keri said you work for an energy company. What do you do?"

"Head of logistics."

"So you tell people where to get stuff when."

"In a nutshell." He slowed as they came into the edge of town.

"Sounds...um, very organized."

"Which in Ella language means boring?"

"You said it, not me." The way she appeared to be trying not to laugh caused him to snort a little as he made the turn into the parking lot for Gia's.

When he held open the front door of the pizzeria for her, her smile lit up her entire face. And damn if he didn't think it was the prettiest thing he'd seen in ages.

"Thanks," she said. "Nice to see the city hasn't robbed you of your chivalry."

"You do know Dallas is still in Texas, right?"

"Really? I hadn't heard."

He smiled and shook his head. Ella Garcia had a lot of sass in that little body of hers, and damn if he didn't like it.

They slid into a booth in the back corner near the

entrance to the kitchen. He took off his hat and placed it in the seat beside him.

"Nice hat, by the way," Ella said. "It suits you."

Maybe it had at one point in his life. "You barely know me."

"I'm decent at pegging people quickly. Comes from never staying any one place too long when I was growing up. It was figure out who to make friends with fast or not have any at all."

"Lot different than going to school with the same people for thirteen years in a row."

"Yeah, foreign concept to me."

The waitress, a little blonde teenager about the size of his pinky finger, came and took their order for a large sausage pizza.

"So, back to the hat," Ella said. "You look at home in it. No interest in becoming a rancher?"

"When I was younger." Back when he'd held out hope that maybe his grandparents would change, would see how the way they chose to live affected him.

"When I was younger, I thought I'd be a fighter pilot when I grew up."

That surprised him. "Really?"

"And then I changed my mind and was determined to become an anthropologist. Then a professional figure skater even though I'd been on ice skates exactly twice. But, hey, it was the year the Winter Olympics were in Nagano, and we were living in Japan. Guess you could say I changed career paths as often as we changed addresses."

"And you settled on making stuff out of other people's junk?"

She sighed. "People are too eager to label things *junk*. We're such a throwaway culture. I like trying to imagine how to give something that's seemingly outlived its usefulness a new life. And lucky for me, there are buyers."

"A lot of them?"

"Enough that I need to figure out how to clone myself. And my house."

His skin itched at the idea that she might be packing her house as full as his grandparents had. "You don't have a shop?"

She shook her head as the waitress placed their drinks on the table then spun to take the order at the next table.

"A little toolshed and the back porch. One of my long-term goals is to be able to buy a place with a lot of room to spread out with storage and work space separate from my house."

He tried to imagine her selling enough reclaimed home decor to afford such a place and had a hard time picturing it. But then he wasn't the most knowledgeable guy about interior decorating or whatever was in style. Somehow he thought his style was probably called minimalist.

"I know a place that will be for sale soon," he said with a little smile that conveyed he knew that probably wasn't in the cards for her.

"Don't think I haven't thought about it. Alas, it's me and the little rental for the foreseeable future. I may see if I can convert the toolshed into a little store if my landlord will let me since they're working to get the arts and crafts trail up and running."

He must have given her a questioning look because she went on to explain.

"The local tourist bureau is compiling a list of all the artists and craftspeople in the area and is going to create a trail with a map so tourists can go from one to the next shopping for handmade items and original art."

"Sounds like a good way to bring in more tourist dollars."

He tried to picture Ella sitting in a little metal toolshed with the name of her business painted on the outside. For some reason, he didn't like the image. She seemed like a hard worker, a go-getter, someone who believed wholeheartedly in what she was doing. Someone like that deserved a better public presence than a place you'd normally store garden tools and lawn mowers.

"If you'd like me to look at a business plan or your work flow plan, let me know."

She stopped with her glass halfway to her mouth. "You'd do that?"

"Yeah. Why do you seem so surprised?"

"Because quite honestly I'm surprised you stopped progress on getting the house ready to sell long enough to come eat, let alone look at the business plan of someone you've known barely more than two seconds."

"It's something I can do easily when I go back to the hotel at night." It was certainly a better use of his time than staring at the ceiling imagining Ella lying in bed next to him. At that thought he had to shift in the booth to make himself less uncomfortable. Thank goodness the table hid what those kinds of thoughts did to him.

"I'll think about it. Thank you for the offer."

"That wasn't meant to say you don't know how to run your business."

She flipped her hand as if to wave away his concern that he'd insulted her.

"Just a little intimidating. I mean, I'm not exactly running a big corporation here."

"Every company starts small." True enough, but a lot of them failed, too. Ella seemed to believe in her business so much, it'd be a shame if hers failed because of lack of proper planning. Sure, he didn't understand her business, but all businesses came down to numbers. And numbers and logistics he understood.

Their pizza arrived, and for a few minutes they abandoned conversation in favor of downing their food. When they got to the last slice, Ella eyed him and pointed at the pizza.

"You going to eat that?"

"No, I'm good."

Unlike most women with whom he'd shared a meal, Ella didn't eat like a little bird. Once she admitted she was hungry, she went about the business of fixing the problem with the same gusto she attacked clearing out his grandparents' house. He admired that she didn't make false pretenses of being full after half a slice.

He found himself wanting to know more about her. Even if he wasn't sticking around Blue Falls for long, it couldn't hurt to be friendly. Especially since they were going to be spending time in close proximity over the next several days.

Austin took a swig of his Coke then placed it back in the ring of condensation on the table. "How did you finally settle on the decor business?"

"Would you believe I fell into it? After all that believing I'd be this or that, my career found me."

"How so?"

She wiped her mouth with her napkin, and he tried like crazy not to think about what the texture of her lips might be like against his own.

"I moved into this apartment in San Antonio where the previous occupant left several boxes of things behind. The owner said he'd take care of getting rid of it, but I managed to talk him into cutting a little off my first month's rent if I did it instead. Well, I found a bunch of old T-shirts, and I ended up making rag rugs and even a woven basket out of them. I painted some old jars and turned them into a chandelier. I liked how the stuff looked in my apartment so much that I was hooked. Granted, that apartment needed all the help it could get."

Ella got a faraway look in her eyes, as if she were back in that apartment filled with what she saw as her recycled treasures. She seemed to come back to the present as she leaned against the back of the red vinyl booth.

"My landlord was so impressed with what I did that he told his wife. She had me make a lighting fixture for their house out of old canning jars. That was my first sale, and I haven't stopped coming up with ideas since."

He could tell by the light in her dark brown eyes that she really did love what she did. He found satisfaction in his job, he was good at it and the position paid well, but he couldn't say that he got out of bed every morning with excitement burning a fire in his veins. But that was unrealistic for most people. He counted it a victory that he didn't hate his job as lots of people did, even a lot of his coworkers.

"I'm still surprised that people seek out things made out of other people's castoffs."

Ella fiddled with the straw in her glass. "Well, I'm glad they do. It's certainly never boring."

"And my job is?"

Ella pretended to nod off and snore. If anyone else had done it, he might have been annoyed. But there was something about her that instead made him laugh. While he liked his job fine, he couldn't sit there and say that sometimes it didn't have its boring days. Ones when he'd stare out the window at the glass and metal and concrete of downtown Dallas and wonder what his life would have been like if he'd followed his boyhood dream of running the ranch.

No sense wondering when he'd never know the answer.

"Austin?"

He looked up to see Ella watching him.

"You went away there for a minute," she said.

"Sorry. The combination of sitting and a full stomach is making me realize how tired I am."

She nodded once. "It's partly the emotional fatigue, too. I've never been so tired in my life as I was in the weeks after my dad died. Just getting up in the morning was exhausting."

"What happened?" he asked, not wanting to think about the loss of his grandfather and the opportunities he'd missed in recent years to put away past disagreements and spend time with the most important person in his life.

Ella picked at the edge of her napkin, shredding little pieces. "He was on a patrol in the mountains of Afghanistan when a Taliban sniper shot him."

Damn. "I'm sorry."

She shrugged as if she'd done it countless times before, the universal symbol of "You can't change the past, no matter how much you might want to."

"How old were you?"

"Fifteen."

"I'm sorry."

Ella's lips quirked up in a slight smile. "You said that already."

"Yeah, well, it bore repeating. It's a crappy hand you were dealt."

"We're all dealt a crappy hand at some point or another."

He knew that firsthand.

"So," she said, sounding a bit tentative, "your grandparents raised you?"

He nodded. "My mother died in a car wreck when I was six months old, and God only knows where my deadbeat of a father is, if he's even still alive, which I wouldn't put money on. My grandparents were the only parents I ever knew."

"It's my turn to say I'm sorry."

He leaned back and rested his arm along the back of the booth. "We're quite the pair, aren't we?"

Ella lifted her glass. "Here's to surviving being dealt crappy hands."

He raised his plastic glass filled with mainly ice and knocked it gently against hers, making a little *thunk* sound. Something inside him felt attracted to her in a new way, and this time it wasn't physical. More the feeling of connection that came from meeting someone with shared experiences, ones the other people in your life couldn't understand because they hadn't lived through it.

The waitress stopped by their table again and placed their ticket on the edge. "No rush. Just whenever you're ready."

"I better get back so I can go unload and come back for another."

He stopped himself before he could tell her that she could wait until the next day because he really did need the place cleaned out quickly. He didn't have endless time off before he had to return to work. As if thinking about work rang the doorbell of the universe, his phone rang and the caller ID revealed it to be his boss. It surprised him to find the interruption annoyed him, a sure sign that he was letting his time back in Blue Falls and with Ella Garcia make him forget what he had to get accomplished in a short amount of time. Making him forget that Ella was nothing more than the woman helping him finally shed the remnants of a past that had weighed on him for too long.

But as he drove them back to the ranch after he finished putting out a logistical fire at work, he couldn't help stealing glances over to her side of the car. Thankfully she was watching the world go by outside the window and didn't notice.

After how they'd talked all the way through their meal, now they had fallen into silence. And at least for him it was a strangely comfortable silence, like there was no pressure to fill it with chitchat.

When he pulled up in front of the house under the big red oak tree, he glanced over to find that Ella appeared to have fallen asleep. And he didn't have the heart to wake her. So he sat, watching the gentle rise and fall of her chest. If she could fall asleep in such a short amount of time, trusting enough to do so with someone she hadn't known long, that told him all he needed to know about how tired she was.

Knowing he shouldn't but seemingly unable to stop himself, he reached over and smoothed her curls away from her face. That she didn't rouse and snap off his fingers gave more evidence that she wasn't getting enough rest.

At that thought, his own fatigue seemed to catch up to him. So he eased his seat back into a partial recline, rolled down the windows so they'd catch the slight early evening breeze and closed his eyes.

Chapter Five

Ella didn't remember leaving a fan running when she went to sleep, but the blowing air fluttered the loose hairs at the side of her face. She reached up to push them away as she opened her eyes. Something about the sight that greeted her didn't sit right in her brain. It wasn't the familiar pale yellow of her bedroom walls or the recovered chair over which she threw her clothes. No, it was…stars?

For a moment, she considered she might be still asleep and dreaming, but then pieces of realization began to coalesce in her mind. Had she…? She turned to her left and saw the sleeping form of Austin Bryant in the reclined driver's seat of his car.

She'd fallen asleep in his car, and instead of disturbing her he'd allowed her to continue to sleep and done the same himself when he could have returned to his much more comfortable bed in his hotel.

Something she couldn't name moved within her, something that felt suspiciously like a deepening of feeling toward this man she didn't really know at all.

Well, she knew enough. He'd been through loss the same as she had. And he wasn't as tough and unfeeling as he might have seemed at first. Sudden affection made an appearance within her, that and a strengthening of the attraction she'd felt toward him from the first moment he'd graced her field of vision.

With Austin asleep, she was able to look as long as she wanted though the light was almost completely gone outside. Her initial impression of rugged, movie star cowboy was only bolstered by how he still looked incredibly sexy while sleeping. She wanted so much to run her hand through his hair and skim her fingers along his jaw. But the moment he awoke, she'd no longer be able to simply watch him without having to avert her eyes.

Yes, they had things in common. And yes, he was so handsome it threatened to steal her breath. But a voice deep within her told her that there was some other indefinable something drawing her toward him.

As she watched him more relaxed than she'd seen him up to this point, a tiny bead of loneliness that she hadn't realized existed grew in size. Its very existence shocked her. She would have denied being lonely if anyone had described her that way, but maybe she'd just been so busy with building her business and getting settled in Blue Falls that she hadn't slowed down enough to notice that little nagging sensation in her middle wasn't only persistent fatigue. But now as she looked at this gorgeous man, the one who perhaps fit on this ranch more than he wanted to admit, she wondered what it would be like if she had someone with whom to share her burdens and laughter and every other little up and down life presented.

She reminded herself he wasn't staying. Not even if she'd caught a couple of longing glances on his face as he'd worked around the ranch earlier. And not even if she was having a hard time picturing him in a suit and tie, sitting in some sterile office in downtown Dallas.

She hadn't been lying when she'd said she was good at pegging people. Sometimes she saw things about them they didn't even realize about themselves, even if that ability obviously didn't work when looking inward. Her gut was rarely wrong about such things, and it was telling her that deep down Austin still longed for that ranching life he'd left far behind.

But it was hard to change paths once you'd invested so much into a chosen career. She couldn't imagine giving up her business and starting all over with something totally different. The very prospect was frightening. She'd make Restoration Decoration a success if it was the last thing she did. Failure wasn't an option, not when she'd seen how it sent life into a tailspin up close and personal. She would not follow in her stepfather Jerry's footsteps, trying and failing at one venture after another.

She shook her head, wondering how admiring Austin's profile had led down a mental path to her never-quite-successful stepfather. Maybe that was her cue to stop staring at Austin and get out of the car before he woke up and things got all kinds of awkward. Before she gave in to the desire to run her fingertips along his strong jaw. It was best she nip her attraction in the bud and keep things between them strictly professional.

Careful not to make too much noise, she eased out of her seat belt and opened the door. With each movement she thought he'd surely wake up. That he didn't was a testament that he was exhausted. Part of her didn't want to leave him out here like this, but she needed some distance between them before she did or said something stupid that she couldn't take back.

Austin was only a temporary part of her life. Soon he'd be back in Dallas, and she'd be in her little house creating decor and furnishing for other people using yet other people's things. In that moment as she closed the passenger door to Austin's car, she realized that after years of living on her own she still didn't have a lot to call hers. Every time she acquired something, she ended up using it on a project she eventually sold or intended to sell. Almost everything she brought into her life just passed through on the way to somewhere and someone else.

So how were things any different from those teenage years when she'd felt alone and lost and grasping for a place that could really feel like a home?

She turned and walked toward her loaded truck, wondering where all the self-reflection with a layer of melancholy had come from. It didn't match the person she'd made of her adult self—the chipper, happy, driven designer and business owner. She'd had enough sad, dark days in her life after her father's death. She was determined not to have any more.

Focusing instead on the vast opportunities the load weighing down her truck presented, she walked away from Austin's car, hoping no critters decided to crawl in through the window to join him. When she reached the truck, she remembered that she hadn't yet tied down her load. Still tired despite her nap, she secured the load with as few tie-downs as she thought she could get by with and slid into the driver's seat.

Austin still hadn't awakened, and for a moment she considered rousing him so he could make his way back to his hotel room. Instead, she let the sounds of her departure do the job for her, slamming the truck's door and starting the engine. When she turned on the headlights, she saw him lift his head. But pretending she hadn't, she put the truck in gear and headed down the driveway with her load of other people's memories.

Austin held up his hand to shade his eyes as a pair of headlights cut through his car. It took a few seconds for him to realize it was Ella leaving with her heavily laden truck. She'd somehow managed to get out of the car without waking him. Was she upset that he'd gone to sleep beside her? It didn't seem like something to be upset over. It wasn't as if he'd lain down beside her on a bed. Not that the idea didn't have more appeal than it should.

He lifted the seat back to its normal position, but instead of starting the car and leaving, he found himself slipping outside and watching as Ella's taillights disappeared beyond the stand of trees blocking the main part of the ranch from the road. He listened as she turned onto the road and headed toward town. Part of him wondered if she'd be back.

Sure she would. There was too much stuff here for her to leave behind. He leaned one hand against the edge of the car's roof and ran his other hand over his face. Why did he have to be so infatuated with someone who couldn't be more opposite of him? She loved the boxes and boxes of what she viewed as possibilities the way he craved the sparse furnishings and lots of empty space in his apartment. She surrounded herself with the leftover pieces of countless other people's

lives while he could fit everything he'd be unwilling
to part with in a single suitcase. If necessary, he could
move with little notice and spent a good bit of time
traveling for work. Ella, on the other hand, seemed
determined to put down roots in a place where she
had none. No, he was the one with roots here and had
thought of little but ripping them up since he'd driven
into town to make funeral arrangements.

He looked toward the silhouette of the house in
the dim light, then the barn, and hated how he'd allowed the disagreements with his grandparents over
their hoarding, even when he'd offered to help them
pare down or get counseling, to overwhelm all the
good times they'd had, the love they'd shown for him,
the way they'd taken him in and raised him as if he
were their own son. He hated how that one point on
which they'd disagreed had pushed him away from
this place.

With a sigh, he headed toward the barn to check on
Duke. He flipped on the lights but didn't immediately
enter the barn. Even though he'd seen all the unnec-
essary items cluttering the interior several times, the
sight still robbed him of breath again. His claustrophobia kicked into high gear, preventing him from
moving any farther inside.

With a glance, he saw that Duke appeared fine.
He'd already been fed his grain for the day, so thankfully didn't need any care that required Austin to enter
the barn more fully. Instead, he turned the lights off
and backed out until he could see the starlit sky above.
It was a gorgeous night, the kind he couldn't fully see
in Dallas. Though he was still tired, he wasn't ready

to go into town and close himself up in a hotel room at the Wildflower Inn.

Though his claustrophobia wasn't so bad that he couldn't stand being in a normally furnished room, right now he wanted nothing more than to breathe fresh air and sit under all that endless sky. He walked several yards away from the barn and climbed up to sit on the top rung of the wooden fence. Most of the ranch's fencing was barbed wire, but along the driveway his grandfather had built a more visually appealing wood-slat fence.

Austin had no idea how many times he'd sat atop this fence wondering how many stars he could see from his little slice of the universe. It had made him long to see more than what could be seen from Blue Falls.

He realized now that the freest he'd ever felt was not in his Dallas office or free-from-clutter apartment. It was right here on this ranch, which was ironic since it was also the place that had made him feel the most trapped.

He thought back to the way Ella's face had glowed while she was talking about her business, her creations, and he wondered if that was how his face had looked whenever he rode out across the ranch. Did he look happy and fulfilled and at home?

Did Ella go outside her house at night and look up at these same stars, marveling at how many there were and how far they extended? Or did she live in town or so close that even Blue Falls' lights obscured part of the celestial show? Maybe she'd seen the stars from so many places around the world that they'd ceased to bring her any sort of awe.

Austin closed his eyes and let the sounds of the summer insects and the warmth of the night tinged with a slightly cooler breeze soak into him. His muscles relaxed, his breathing slowed and his mind eased. He had lots to do in the days ahead, but for this one moment he was going to just be and enjoy something he'd almost allowed himself to forget—being at peace in the great outdoors.

The longer he sat, the louder the whisper in his mind became when it asked why he was going to leave this behind for a second time.

Because no matter how much he might want to, there was no going back in time and making different decisions. Instead, you dealt with the ones you made and kept moving forward.

Right back out of Blue Falls, off this ranch, away from a petite, curly-haired brunette who made him wonder things he shouldn't be wondering.

ELLA TOOK A big swig of her Coke as she pulled into the driveway for the ranch the next morning. She needed the caffeine after another late night of working, but it was already too blasted hot for coffee.

And as if she wasn't already hot enough, when she spotted Austin up on her ladder scraping old paint off the side of the house, the T-shirts he'd been wearing had given way to a tank-style undershirt that showed off his arms nicely. Damn, how did a man who worked in an office have arms like that?

As she backed her truck toward the front of the house, she told herself she wasn't going to ogle Austin when she stepped out. After waking up sleeping next to him the night before, the last thing she needed was something else to add to the pile o' awkward.

Seemed her hormones had different ideas, though, because the moment she shut her door, her gaze went right to him in all his sweaty, muscled glory. Images of doing sweaty things with him popped into her mind, causing her face to flame. Thank goodness she wasn't fair-skinned.

"Morning," he said as he wiped his forehead with his right forearm.

"Good morning. Going to be a hot one." *State the obvious much?*

"Already there."

"Make sure you drink enough water." And…now she sounded like someone's mother.

The smile that nudged up the edge of his mouth darn near had her moaning out loud. She suddenly wondered if he was seeing anyone, and if it was okay for her to hate the woman without having ever met her.

Before she could open her mouth and make an even bigger fool of herself, she made for the front door. Once inside and out of view of Austin, she rolled her eyes at herself. She was here to do a job, not pant after a guy simply because he looked good in a tank. Okay, *really* good.

Cognizant of how Austin wanted the house emptied quickly, she sped up her logging process using abbreviations instead of more detailed descriptions. She just hoped she could remember what everything meant later. Making her way through another section of the master bedroom, she occasionally came across things that seemed as if they ought to mean something to Austin. Instead of asking him about them and getting the same "I don't want anything" answer, she started putting them in a box in the corner she'd cleared out. When she was done with everything, she'd ask him one last time about them.

The sound of scraping outside the window drew her attention. The sight of Austin's torso in that white undershirt made her mouth water so much she considered going outside and sticking her head below the spigot again. She knew she should look away and get back to work, but she couldn't. It'd been a long time since she'd been with anyone, and her body was screaming at her that it was time to end the drought. But she couldn't exactly go outside and say, "Hey, Austin. You look mighty hot up there. Why don't you come down here and let me help you out of those clothes?"

She forced herself to turn her back to the window, but not even going through boxes like she was digging for buried treasure was able to steer her mind away from the sexy man working just on the other side of the wall. And that was saying something.

Somehow she managed to keep making progress throughout the morning, letting herself glance casually out the window at Austin's very fine body only every few minutes. She had a feeling that fantasies about this man would linger long after he'd sold this place and gone back to his life in Dallas.

Shaking her head, she grabbed a box of costume jewelry and embroidered linens she'd finished logging and headed out to the truck. As she stepped out onto the porch, she nearly collided with Austin. He veered just in time to prevent getting a box to the stomach.

"Sorry," she said. "Thought you were still up on the ladder."

"Taking a break. Someone told me I needed to keep hydrated." He leaned down and picked up a large bottle of water. As he took a long drink, she couldn't manage to tear her gaze away. Was there anything sexier than a sweaty, good-looking man in a shirt that adhered to his chest, jeans hanging at just the right spot to make her think about taking them off, scuffed cowboy boots—where had those come from?—and topped off by a cowboy hat that looked so perfect on him she would swear he'd never stepped foot off this ranch?

It was as if her brain had received a jolt of electricity, rendering her temporarily mute, because she hadn't the foggiest idea how to respond. As if the universe was taking pity on her, she heard the crunch of gravel on the driveway and turned to see a small silver car heading toward the house.

"Expecting company?" she finally managed to say.

"Nope." Austin took another long drink of water and moved to the edge of the porch. When he braced one forearm against a support pillar, it was all she could do not to moan out loud. Honestly, the man should come with a big, blinking warning label that said, "May cause extreme hot flashes and naughty thoughts."

She peeled her gaze away from him as the car stopped and the driver's side door opened. When Verona Charles stepped out, she couldn't stop the single curse word she muttered under her breath.

Austin looked over at her. "Something wrong?"

Not wrong, precisely. "You know how every small

town has that one person who thinks they know what's best for everyone else?" She nodded in Verona's direction as the older woman pulled something from the passenger seat of her car.

"She's the one who suggested I contact you," he said.

"So I heard."

He appeared as though he was about to ask something else, but he was prevented from doing so by Verona's approach.

"Hey, you two," Verona said with a wave and a big smile that should be accompanied by its own warning sign.

"Ms. Charles," Austin said as he pushed away from the pillar and descended the steps. "What brings you all the way out here?"

Verona flicked her fingers in a dismissive gesture. "None of that 'Ms. Charles' stuff. Call me Verona like everyone else does." She lifted a large white paper bag with a pink primrose on the side and the words *Primrose Café* in a pretty script. It looked way prettier than the homespun atmosphere at the Primrose would suggest.

"The Primrose is trying out a new picnic lunch idea with plans to launch it in conjunction with the beginning of the arts and crafts trail if all goes well." She tapped her fingers against the side of the bag. "They need some test subjects to try it out, and I thought of you two out here working up an appetite."

Austin looked genuinely confused, which almost made Ella laugh out loud. Verona wasn't what one would call subtle in her matchmaking efforts. But

Austin hadn't lived here in so long that he probably hadn't gotten that particular memo.

"You must have read my mind," Ella said, pretending like she hadn't a clue what Verona was up to. "I'm starving." She hurried down the steps to take the bag from the other woman.

"Um, what do I owe you?" Austin asked as he reached for the wallet in his back pocket.

"Not a penny. Just stop by the Primrose and tell them what you think of the meal when you get the chance. Maybe you'll like it so much that you will decide to grab dinner while you're there." Verona had a sparkle in her eyes that telegraphed for anyone to see that she was proud of her efforts. "You could even request another lunch like this and have it down by the lake."

"Is retirement getting boring and you've taken a job with the Primrose?" Ella asked, barely suppressing a smile.

"Nah, just helping out friends when I can."

Uh-huh. Ella might not be a native of Blue Falls, but she knew Verona's tactics well enough to know that she'd more than likely fed the idea of the picnic lunches to the Primrose's owners with the sole purpose of being able to bring one out here to Ella and Austin.

"Well, gotta run. You two enjoy your lunch."

"Thanks," Austin said, sounding every bit as confused as he looked.

As Verona retraced her steps to her car and slipped into the driver's seat, Austin turned partly toward Ella.

"I know Blue Falls is a friendly town, but this

seems out of the ordinary." He pointed toward the bag in Ella's hands.

"Not for Verona." She hesitated before filling him in when her mind shifted back to the thoughts she'd been having about him only a few minutes ago. "Let's just say that retirement has given her more time to indulge her favorite pastime, matchmaking."

Austin glanced toward where Verona's car was disappearing beyond the tree line. "So, she's…"

Feeling the heat rising in her cheeks again, Ella directed her attention to the contents of the bag. "Don't worry about it. You'll be gone soon and she'll move on. Now, I don't know about you, but I'm not letting a perfectly good free lunch go to waste."

Ella turned and headed up the steps. When she realized that Austin wasn't following her, she stopped and turned halfway back toward him. "Are you not hungry?"

"I'm fine."

She lifted an eyebrow. "Now who's fibbing about not being hungry?"

He huffed a little laugh. "Busted."

Ella set the bag on the edge of the porch. "Be right back." She went inside to where she'd seen a stack of patchwork quilts. Hoping the sight of one didn't upset him, she grabbed it and a couple of bottles of water she'd stored in the fridge, then went back outside.

"Seems if we've got a picnic lunch, we ought to really have a picnic, don't you think?" She descended the steps, leaving the bag filled with the food for him to carry, and walked toward a spot under the trees at the edge of the yard.

As she spread out the quilt on the ground, she tried

to tell herself this was no big deal, that she wasn't allowing herself to be pulled into Verona's plan. This was simply two people, coworkers of a sort, eating a meal at the same time at the same place—no different from when they'd eaten pizza at Gia's after a hard day of work. But there was that part of her that did think this was romantic and perhaps wished it could be more. It would be nice to at least be able to explore if more could develop between them, but it didn't make sense to go down a road she knew led to a dead end.

Austin stopped at the edge of the quilt and looked down at her. "You can eat inside, where it's cooler."

"No, this will be fun. I haven't had an actual picnic like this since I was a little girl."

When Austin finally sat across from her, she questioned the wisdom of being this close to him. How was she supposed to concentrate on eating food when he was what really looked yummy?

"Smells good," he said.

It took her a moment to realize he was talking about the food. Yeah, this meal was going to be a challenge to get through.

She started pulling carefully wrapped food from the bag and arranging it on the quilt between them.

"So what did you do to get on Verona's matchmaking list?" Austin asked.

Ella looked up from where she was placing what looked like a container of corkscrew pasta on the quilt. "You mean other than not have a ring on my left hand? Nothing. Be glad you're leaving soon."

A brief look passed across Austin's face that Ella couldn't quite identify, but it did something funny to her middle.

"You say that like I'd think the pairing was awful or something," he said.

What was he saying?

"No, but I think people ought to get to choose who they want to pair up with, don't you? Plus, Verona often jumps in without all the facts. Like she couldn't possibly know if you have a girlfriend back in Dallas."

Had she just said that? Did it sound like fishing to him as much as it did to her own ears? Trying not to let it show that she was worried about what she'd just said, she pulled out thick sandwiches and a container of various berries.

"Maybe I should start the rumor that I do."

Rumor? Did that mean he wasn't dating anyone? That thought made her ridiculously happy when it shouldn't matter at all.

"Oh, sure. Throw me under the matchmaking bus."

"It's every man for himself."

Her mouth dropped open, and when Austin laughed she grabbed a strawberry and threw it at him.

"Hey, that's a perfectly good strawberry," he said as he bobbled then caught it in his hand.

"Be glad something heavier and pointier wasn't handy."

He just smiled and brought the strawberry to his mouth. When he took a bite then licked the juice from his lips, she knew the universe was torturing her for some reason. Because, man, was she jealous of that strawberry.

Austin grabbed one of the sandwiches, and she couldn't help but watch his hands as they made quick work of the paper wrapping. She imagined those hands rubbing down the horse in the barn, handling the reins as he rode out among the herd of cattle, clasping the hem of that white shirt and pulling it over his head to reveal the mysteries that lay beneath.

Skimming over her naked flesh.

Good grief, her hormones were having a no-holds-barred party.

"Mmm, this is pretty good," he said as he held up the roasted turkey sandwich. "Maybe we should mess with Verona so she'll bring us one of these lunches every day."

Ella snorted. "This is good, but definitely not worth encouraging her. We do that and she'll be announcing our engagement in the paper."

She might be joking on the outside, but something about saying those words made Ella feel jittery inside, as though part of her maybe even liked the idea. How much sense did that make, thinking of happily-ever-after with someone she'd just met? *That's right, none at all.*

They fell into silence as they ate, just as they had at Gia's, and Ella was surprised at how comfortable it was, even though she was still hyperaware of her intense attraction to Austin, especially when he leaned back on one elbow and stretched out his long legs.

She glanced over at him and caught him rubbing the pad of his forefinger across one of the swatches of cloth making up the quilt.

"You remember that fabric?" she asked.

He glanced up in a way that made her think he hadn't realized that he'd been transported back in time.

"Yeah. It's from one of my grandmother's blouses. I remember this old dog we had pulled it out of the laundry basket and turned it into a chew toy. Never one to waste anything, she cut up the rest of the fabric and put it into quilts like this one." A slight smile tugged at the edge of his mouth, one that was part fond memory and part sadness. "You two would have probably gotten along like two peas in a pod."

She got the impression he'd had some sort of falling out with his grandparents, but he'd still loved them. That he would say what he did touched her more than he'd probably intended.

"So what would you make with something like this?" He poked the quilt with that same finger.

She thought about it for a moment then ran her hand over a section that was less worn. "I'd take the better parts and make things like throw pillows and pin cushions. I'd have to study how first, but I bet I could make a jacket out of it, too."

"What would you charge for products like that?"

Again, she had to consider his question before tossing out figures.

"And people pay that?"

"Yeah. Handmade quilts are popular, even if they're no longer used as quilts."

"Then I'm glad you're taking all this stuff."

"Because it will be given a new life?"

"Yeah, I guess. And help you build your business."

Warmth spread throughout her chest. "Thank you."

He shrugged. "It's better it be used than just sit stacked in corners for decades."

There it was, that layer of frustration that had been apparent from the moment he'd shown her into the house.

"Can I ask you something?"

When he met her eyes, she thought for a moment he'd say no. But instead he gave a slight nod.

"Your grandfather seemed like a nice man, and yet you don't want to keep anything that has to do with your grandparents. I gather you had a strained relationship because of the hoarding?"

"By the time I moved away for college, yeah, things were pretty strained. I couldn't understand why they were so resistant to getting rid of stuff, and they didn't understand why it all bothered me." He placed the uneaten portion of his sandwich on the wrapper and looked toward the house. "It was embarrassing, for one thing."

"Because you couldn't have friends over."

He glanced at her, seemingly surprised that she understood.

"After my dad died, we went through some pretty lean years," she said, remembering all too well that burning desire to grow up and move out on her own. "When we first moved to Texas, let's just say our apartment was a dump. I used to get off the bus at the public library and walk from there because I didn't want anyone to know where I lived."

"But things turned around?"

"For a while. My mom got remarried. We moved a lot as my stepfather tried one thing and then another, unfortunately not really succeeding at any of them." Ella moved her pasta salad around with her plastic fork. "I think seeing that is part of the reason I want my business to succeed so much."

"From what I've seen of how driven you are, you should."

She smiled. "I appreciate that."

Only a few days ago, Ella would have said all she really wanted was to build a successful business doing what she loved and to eventually get a little place of her own. Now, as she sat eating a picnic lunch with Austin, she realized that there was something else she wanted, too. But it was the one thing she couldn't have no matter how hard she worked.

Chapter Six

Over the next few days, Austin worked on prepping the rest of the exterior of the house for painting and was surprised he didn't mind all the manual labor. In fact, he found his body craving it, as if he'd been denied food for a decade and had suddenly been plunked down at a king's feast.

He knew he had to go back to Dallas, his job, his life, but with each passing day he could feel more of himself reattaching to this ranch. With every step he took toward being able to list it for sale, the more the idea of letting it go didn't sit well. He found himself adding to his to-do list, prolonging the time necessary to complete the tasks. He wasn't so blind that he didn't realize part of the reason also had to do with Ella.

Since that first day they'd eaten the picnic Verona had brought them, they'd fallen into eating lunch together, either sitting on the front steps or sometimes back on the old patchwork quilt under the trees. He knew it would be much more comfortable in the air-conditioning, but he didn't want to spoil this time he was able to spend back on the ranch by going inside and seeing all the things that had driven him away.

Their lunch conversations since that first day had

been about easier topics than the past—everything from the fact that neither of them had pets, mainly because they were too busy to care for them, to favorite ice cream flavors. Even though he grew more attracted to her each day, it also felt as if they were becoming good friends. He had friends in Dallas, but none of them knew much about his background. The fact that Ella now knew more than all of them put together and didn't appear to think any less of him only made him feel more drawn to her.

Which he knew was a bad idea. He couldn't start something with her when he wasn't staying. It might be nice to take this side trip down memory lane, to revisit the parts of his youth he'd enjoyed, but the reality was that his job wasn't going to wait forever. He had responsibilities, commitments he couldn't just ignore or pass off to someone else while he played rancher.

"You seem deep in thought," Ella said from where she sat cross-legged on the opposite side of the quilt.

"Just wondering what color I should paint the house that would make it appealing to potential buyers." He looked over at her. "What do you think?"

She cocked her head at an angle and stared at the house. "What about a limestone-type color? It would match a lot of the actual stone exteriors of houses around here."

He directed his gaze at the house where he'd grown up, trying to imagine it a color other than the dusty greenish-brown it had always been. Finally, he nodded. "I like it."

"So you're really going to sell the place?"

"Yeah. You sound surprised."

She leaned back on her palms. "I kind of am.

You've relaxed a lot since you've been here. I even heard you whistling while you were working earlier."

"It's nice to have a break from my normal routine."

"No, that's not it."

He lifted an eyebrow. "Oh, really?"

"Remember what I said about being able to peg people? You love this place. Maybe it has some stressful, perhaps even unhappy memories, but you seem at home here."

She was echoing a voice that had begun to whisper at the back of his mind the past few days, but it had to be nostalgia trying to tempt him into believing that he could go back, could do things differently. But what was done was done, and soon this ranch would fall into that category.

"I won't lie and say that it doesn't have some appeal, but I can't just give up everything I've worked for. Ranching isn't an easy job. It's hard to make it work financially."

"Your grandfather made it work."

"Did he? He would have had to sell off the herd this year just to make the tax payment on the ranch."

"Oh." Ella looked out across the pasture. "Will you sell the herd with the ranch?"

"If the buyer wants the cattle, yeah, that would be easier. If not, I'll try to sell them to another rancher."

"How big is the ranch? Wait, never mind. I'm not good at being able to even picture how big an acre is."

"I can show you if you're willing to help me string a bit of fencing."

"Wow, you're taking this free-labor thing a bit far, don't you think?"

He laughed. "Can't blame a guy for trying."

Ella leaned forward and wrapped her arms around her upturned knees. "I could do that, provided you realize I have no idea what I'm doing. Not a lot of call for learning how to string barbed wire living in base housing."

And so after they finished their lunch, he put work on the house on hold and loaded the supplies he needed into his grandfather's old pickup truck. He retrieved an extra set of work gloves from the barn and handed them to Ella. She slipped them on and they swallowed her hands.

"Well, these are all kinds of sexy."

Man, he wished the woman wouldn't say the word *sexy*, because it had him thinking about peeling off those gloves along with everything else she was wearing and stretching her out on that quilt in the shade.

Maybe asking her to go with him had been a really bad idea. Nope, no *maybe* about it.

"You'll be glad you have them in a few minutes."

When they slipped into the old pickup, the cab smelled like his grandfather—a combination of the aftershave with the faux forest scent, leather and lemon hard candies. Austin couldn't remember a time when his grandfather didn't have those candies close at hand.

As he drove along the dirt road that skirted the edge of the ranch, he remembered how many times he'd taken this same path for the same reason. Only those times he'd been in the passenger seat, where Ella now sat.

"So, how's it going in the house?" he asked, needing to talk about something that would take his mind off how beautiful she was without even trying. It was as if each day he saw her more clearly, her beauty increasing.

He needed to get the ranch ready to sell and get the heck out of Blue Falls before he gave in to his attraction and did something that might cause her to knock him into next week.

"Fine. I can speed up if you need me to."

"No, that wasn't why I asked." If she worked any harder, she was going to collapse or drive off the side of the road on the way home. So why was he dragging her out to the back of the ranch to string fencing?

Oh yeah, because he liked being around her. And he was evidently selfish enough to add to her long day just so they could spend more time together.

"How long before you have to leave?" she asked.

"I've got another week of time off, unless some logistical emergency arises."

"I don't know how you do it, going into an office where someone else dictates when you work, when you eat, when you can go home. I just don't think I'm built that way."

He had to admit that making his own schedule, even if he was working hard, had been nice the past several days. It might require long days, but there was a freedom in ranch work that he'd managed to forget. Returning to working within four man-made walls was going to be more difficult than he would have imagined.

"It's not all in an office. I travel, spend time on job sites."

"Somehow I doubt an oil field is as pretty as it is out here."

She had him there.

"How long has this ranch been in your family?"

He rested his arm along the edge of the open window, breathing in the scent of sun-baked earth. "I guess you could say three generations, though my mom never really had much to do with it."

"Shame to see it go, though I guess that happens all the time."

True, but it still didn't prevent the knot that started forming in his chest. He tried not to think about another family living in his childhood home, riding across these pastures, taking in these views. It didn't seem right, and yet holding on to a place he didn't intend to work didn't make much sense.

When they reached the area that needed a new string of barbed wire, he stopped the truck and hopped out. By the sound of the closing door, Ella had followed suit. When a few of the herd grazing nearby looked toward them, Ella stepped over to the fence.

"Hey, there. Aren't you some handsome fellas."

Austin chuckled. "You do know they're going to end up as steaks on someone's plate, right?"

"Shh," she said as she motioned for him to be quiet, then looked back toward the cattle. "Don't pay him any mind. He doesn't know what he's talking about."

An unexpected light feeling filled Austin's chest. It was almost impossible to feel down with Ella around. Considering the sadness she'd endured with her father's death and the subsequent years of lean times and constant moving, it was a bit of a miracle she was so cheerful and fun to be around. In that moment, he wished things could be different. Wished Dallas were closer to Blue Falls so he could take a chance and ask her out. He'd still be far enough away that should she shoot him down, he wouldn't have to see her. But if she said yes? Then they could make dating work.

But Dallas wasn't close to Blue Falls, so it was a waste of time to play that what-if game.

"Come on, Cattle Whisperer," he said as he pulled the roll of barbed wire out of the back of the truck. As he got a new strand of wire in place and started to use the stretcher, he motioned Ella back several steps. "You don't want to be too close if it pops loose. That could ruin your day."

"Safety advice from the guy who headbutted a rain gutter."

"In my defense, I'd never worked on gutters before. Fencing, that I've done."

He used the fence stretcher to pull the wire tight. "Come here and lean against this while I nail."

She moved into position against the stretcher, and he was half-surprised she had enough body weight to hold the wire tight. He pulled the U-shaped fence staples from his pocket and made quick work of securing the new wire. They moved on down the fence, working well together. He faltered only when he looked up and saw Ella watching not the cows, not the surrounding landscape, not even the fence, but him. Her gaze was fixed somewhere around his biceps, at least until she realized he was looking at her.

For a brief moment, their gazes locked and he'd swear he saw the same raw interest in her eyes that he'd been feeling toward her the past several days. That look could spell trouble for both of them.

Ella finally broke eye contact, and damn if he didn't want it back. That and more.

ELLA WAS PRETTY sure the heat flooding her had
nothing to do with the sun beating down on them
and everything to do with how good Austin looked
doing manual labor. There was just something about
a man's well-defined biceps that got to her. If she'd
been able to see his chest as well, she'd have been a
goner and probably would have launched herself at
him, knocking him down and collapsing on top of
him, heedless of the rocks and all manner of things
that could poke and scratch their skin.

So she didn't act on those impulses, instead looking down and fixing her gaze on the large gloves she
was wearing and frantically searching for a topic of
conversation that had nothing to do with pure animal attraction.

"How old were you when you first did this?"

The amount of time it took Austin to answer had
Ella wondering if he might be feeling as knocked off-
kilter as she was at the moment.

"Can't remember. Had to be in elementary school,
though I was working on the ranch as far back as I
can remember."

"Born rancher, eh?"

Austin moved on to the next section of fencing
and stretched the wire like a pro. "Almost. I was actually born in Houston, but I was still a baby when I
came to live here."

"That's when...your mom passed?"

He nodded. "She'd dropped me off with a baby-
sitter and was on her way to work. A guy ran a red
light and T-boned her. I choose to think she never saw
it coming and didn't know it happened."

Before she thought about it, Ella reached out and

placed her gloved hand against his forearm. "I'm sorry. At least I got several years with my dad, got to know him."

"I'm not sure your experience isn't worse. I mean, there's a love there for my mom because she was my mom, but it's a distant sort of thing since I don't remember her. To love someone until you're almost an adult only to have them ripped away, that seems way worse."

Maybe he was right. Neither experience was enviable.

"So did you have a favorite part of growing up on a ranch?"

"Just being outside, riding out to the far edges of the property."

She leaned against the stretching tool again as he hammered the nails into the post to secure the new wire. "Do you still get to ride?"

He rested his forearm atop the fence post. "Before the other day, I hadn't been on a horse in several years."

"Must be like riding a bike, then, because you seemed right at home in the saddle."

He stared into the distance without speaking for several long seconds. "It felt good to do it again."

She wanted to ask him why he would leave this place and way of life a second time when it was so obvious that he loved it. Could the memories of the strain and disagreement between him and his grandparents be so strong that they overshadowed the good parts? Or was it that he was too entrenched in his life to contemplate making a change? But she didn't ask those questions. With how she was feeling toward him, the last thing she needed to do was delve deeper into his feelings, ones that were so deeply rooted that it didn't make sense to share them with someone you'd known only a few days. Plus, she wasn't entirely sure she wanted him to stay, for him or for her.

After a few minutes of quiet, she steered the conversation toward less emotionally wrought topics. "Since you're in town, you going to the rodeo tomorrow night?"

"Didn't even know about it."

"You should go. I bet you could catch up with some old friends, get away from work for a few hours."

He smiled a little. "This your way of getting a night off?"

"Hardly. I'm working my booth." At his questioning look, she continued. "We always have a sort of flea market/bazaar deal at the fairgrounds the nights of the rodeo. It's a good way to get my work in front of new people."

"Tourists? They come to the rodeos?"

"They do. They go shopping or boating on the lake or on one of the wildflower tours during the day, then hit the rodeo at night. The attendance has been growing a lot in the past year. And the proceeds after expenses always go to a good cause." She reached up and shoved some loose tendrils of hair out of her eyes. "This time it's actually going to build more grandstands and bathroom facilities at the fairgrounds to accommodate the larger crowds."

"I don't think I have time to waste going to socialize with people I haven't hung out with in years. I have to get back to my real job soon, and the hours are ticking away."

Something that felt too much like dread twisted inside Ella. In such a short time, she'd gotten used to seeing Austin every day, eating lunch with him, chatting about so many different topics she'd lost count. She realized that since he'd called her to come clean out his grandparents' belongings, she'd not done anything with her friends. When she wasn't home unloading, sleeping or getting ready to head to the ranch, she was here with Austin. Each morning, anticipation sizzled inside her as she drew closer to the ranch and seeing Austin again.

She knew the best thing was for him to go back to Dallas before she really allowed her infatuation to run away with itself, but she didn't want him to.

"Speaking of time ticking away, I really need to get back to work so I can go home and finish prepping for the rodeo market." Oh, and complete the tractor wheel table. She'd never been late on a project delivery date before, not even when she had the flu, and she didn't intend to start now.

They made quick work of the final three stretches of wire, then tossed the leftover wire and the tools in the back of the truck. As Austin drove them back toward the main part of the ranch, Ella watched out her window and wondered what it was like to own this much land. She knew this ranch was small potatoes compared with some in Texas, but it still seemed enormous and wonderful to someone who had yet to own any real estate of her own. Or even live on a slice that was bigger than a postage stamp.

"Will you be here tomorrow?" Austin asked as he parked next to her truck.

"In the morning, unless I'm running out of time

here. Then I'll make it work to be here longer." Somehow. She tried not to think about how at some point she was going to hit the wall and not be able to keep going on determination alone.

Austin stared out the windshield for a long moment. "I've got to be done with everything by the end of next week. I can't put off going back to work any longer than that."

A week? He'd be gone in a week, and she very likely wouldn't ever see him again. If he no longer had family or property in Blue Falls, he had no reason to come back. Certainly not to see someone he'd simply worked in close proximity to for a couple of weeks.

Don't focus on him. Focus on the job.

After all, that was why she was here, not to appreciate the physical attributes of one Austin Bryant.

"Okay." For some reason, she couldn't say anything more than that single-word acknowledgment.

On her drive home, she turned the radio up loud and sang along to the rock songs to try to stop thinking about how much she'd miss seeing Austin every day. What the heck was wrong with her? Wasn't she too old to get burning-hot crushes like this?

Even the double scoop of chocolate brownie ice cream she stopped to get in town didn't take her mind off its fixation. Neither did pouring all her energy into working on the tractor wheel table.

As daylight started to fade, she sank onto the edge of her back porch, totally spent. She'd give a fortune if she had it to be able to curl up in bed and sleep for three days straight. Instead, she stared at the still-loaded truck and thought about everything that was still at the Bryant ranch. Where in the world was she going to put it? Maybe she could get a decent deal on a storage unit. She needed more space in the worst sort of way. If she just knew that business would continue to build, she'd have no qualms about forking over enough to pay for storage. But she'd seen the consequences of overestimating one's future success, and she didn't want to make that same mistake. She had to remember the old adage that slow and steady was the way to win the race.

But those were hard words to live by when she had such big dreams, so many ideas that her head could barely contain them all.

Just like it was hard to remember that having the serious hots for a guy passing through her life wasn't her best idea either.

AUSTIN MADE HIS way to a table next to the wall in the Primrose Café. He hadn't eaten dinner the night before, too tired and his head filled with too much confusion to even think about food. Consequently, he was starving this morning.

The waitress arrived with a pot of coffee and took his order for pancakes with a side of bacon. Someone patted him on the back before sliding into the chair opposite him.

Austin huffed out a laugh at the sight of Simon Teague in a sheriff's department uniform. "Even though I'd heard you were sheriff, this," he said, motioning toward Simon's attire, "still doesn't compute."

Simon smiled. "Yeah, I get that a lot. So, how go things out at the ranch? I heard Ella Garcia is helping you clear the place out."

That's right, Simon would know about the hoarding. He'd been called out to the ranch a couple of years ago when someone had tried to steal his grandfather's truck. At least until his grandfather probably made the guy soil his drawers with a well-placed shot that took out one of his own tires. It cost him a tire, but got rid of the thief lickety-split.

"Yeah. She says she can use all the stuff my grandparents accumulated, and I'm just glad to get rid of it."

"From what I hear, she's building a following. I know Keri and her friends like Ella's work."

Austin still couldn't picture it, but to each his—or her—own.

"How long you in town for?" Simon asked.

"Just a few more days, enough time to get the place in decent enough shape to sell."

"So you're not staying?"

Austin shook his head, a little surprised by how hard it was to do so. After the initial resistance to being back in the spot that had caused strife between him and the two people he'd loved most in the world, he'd fallen back into the rhythm of ranch life with such ease it had scared him a little. He was still drawn to it, but that life was in his past. A person didn't just walk away from everything he'd worked hard for in order to try to recapture a long-ago dream. And that's all it was, a dream. Ranching had changed so much since he was a kid. Each year it became harder to make it as a small operation.

"So life is treating you well in Dallas?"

Was there a hint of disbelief in Simon's voice? No, Austin had to be imagining it.

"Yeah. Can't complain."

"That's good. Though if you ever change your mind, Blue Falls would always welcome you back."

Austin placed his coffee cup back on the table after taking a drink. "You're just wanting to increase the number of law-abiding citizens."

Simon chuckled. "There is that. Though can't say we're overrun with crime here, which makes my job a lot more pleasant than my comrades' in bigger cities."

For some reason, Austin thought about the previous fall, when a vandal had been going around keying the paint on parked cars in Austin's neighborhood. Unfortunately, his car had been one of the victims. He couldn't imagine that happening in Blue Falls.

He had to stop comparing the two. This wasn't some mushy movie about going home again and recapturing the past. Maybe that happened occasionally in real life, but it was way more prevalent in nostalgic fiction.

"I heard from my grandfather that you married Keri Mehler. Didn't see that coming either."

"Me neither, but sometimes that kind of thing sneaks up on you when you're least expecting it."

An image of Ella spreading out his grandmother's quilt on the ground for one of their lunches had him gripping his cup a bit harder. He consciously released it but then saw a look on Simon's face that reminded him a little too much of the glee on Verona's face as she'd left them with the picnic lunch. That reminded him that he needed to give someone here at the Primrose his review.

When the waitress returned with his breakfast, he shared with her how much he'd liked the picnic fixings.

She looked at him with confusion. "I'd not heard we were doing anything like that."

"Verona Charles said she was trying to help out the owners by getting some feedback."

Simon started laughing at the same time the waitress smiled and touched Austin's forearm.

"I think that basket had more to do with Verona's goals than anyone's here," the waitress said.

When she walked away, Simon was bringing his laughter under control. Barely. "Keri was right. Verona has you in her matchmaking crosshairs, you and Ella. Welcome back to Blue Falls and its main peril."

Austin cut into his pancakes. "Gotta say it doesn't make much sense to try to fix up someone who doesn't live here."

"Oh, you don't know Verona well. She's convinced her powers of matchmaking are so good that a little thing like not living here won't be a problem for long. And based on what I've seen, she's not wrong."

Austin looked across the table. "You know, meddling neighbors isn't exactly a selling point for trying to get people to move here."

"What? It's quaint. People love quaint."

Austin snorted.

As Austin ate and Simon drank a cup of coffee, they talked about their high school days, what former classmates were up to now. Austin noted how the majority of them were married and had kids. Well, except for local mechanic Greg Bozeman. But that wasn't surprising for someone who'd been a colossal flirt since he'd hit puberty.

"You should come out to the rodeo tonight," Simon said. "The whole Teague gang will be there. I guarantee you'll know a lot of other people, too. Catch up before you head back to the big city."

"You sound like Ella."

"Really? She invited you to the rodeo? Maybe Verona is right."

"She was just being friendly." But he wondered. He'd replayed that moment out by the fence too many times to count. That look in her dark eyes had caused a jolt of adrenaline to rush through him.

"Uh-huh. You could do worse, you know. She's a nice person, and pretty."

"Keri know you go around praising other women's looks?"

"My wife would say the same thing."

Austin rolled his eyes, thinking Verona must be rubbing off on the other residents.

"Plus I heard they were looking for someone to fill in as another pickup cowboy tonight, too," Simon said. "One of the normal guys can't be here. His wife just had a baby last night."

"It's been forever since I did anything like that. Heck, this past week was the first time I'd been on a horse in forever."

"Pfftt, it's like riding a bike."

Austin opened his mouth, about to say Simon sounded like Ella again, but then thought better of it. "I've still got a lot of work to do and not much time to do it."

"Suit yourself." Simon stood. "Well, got to go ride herd on the criminal element."

Austin smiled at the thought of Blue Falls having much of a "criminal element."

As he drove out toward the ranch after finishing his breakfast, he took his time. Though he knew he couldn't actually do it, he wondered what it would

be like to live in Blue Falls again. He'd liked growing up here, would have probably stayed if not for the
ugly scene with his grandparents that first Christmas
break from college.

No, he didn't want to think about that. He waved at
Jasper Clark, who was riding an ATV along the edge
of his property. When Austin reached the point in the
road about a mile from where he'd turn into the ranch,
a spot that afforded an unobstructed view to the west,
he pulled over on the edge of the road. Texas didn't
get any prettier than this, in his opinion. Yes, he'd be
going back home in a few days, resuming his regular
life, and he had a ton to do before then, but that didn't
mean he couldn't try to enjoy some of his time here.
Maybe he would go to the rodeo tonight. He'd catch
up with old friends, soak up some of the country life,
watch a good, old-fashioned rodeo.

And if he happened to catch a few glimpses of a
certain pretty brunette, well, that was just a bonus.

Chapter Seven

Ella hurried to get her booth set up at the edge of the field adjacent to the rodeo grounds. Already people were beginning to wander through the surrounding booths, and here she was, rushing as usual, playing catch-up.

After oversleeping that morning, she'd had to move fast to get a small load of things from Austin's ranch, clearing out what was left in the bathroom and one of the bedrooms. She didn't even attempt to log the items. The end of the week was going to arrive in no time.

Not crossing paths with Austin much while she'd been there was probably a good thing. It would help her begin to pull away, to get her mind back where it belonged, building her business and securing her future. He'd been busy meeting with another area rancher who'd come by to talk to him about possibly acquiring his herd. Something about that—another person coming by to possibly take things away from this ranch—made his leaving more real than his words had.

She was thankful the rodeo market was tonight, giving her interaction with customers and reminding her that her time at the Bryant ranch was only a sourcing job, nothing more.

Then why did telling herself that feel like a lie?

She pulled herself up into the bed of her truck and shoved a table made from an old door and two up-turned car rims, all painted a distressed robin's egg blue, toward the tailgate. She had to be careful get-ting it out of the truck or risk damaging it. But she'd learned from experience that leaving anything in the truck to make transport easier discouraged buyers.

Ella grunted as she pushed.

"Need a hand?"

Her breath caught when she looked up and saw Austin, looking more like a real, honest-to-God cow-boy than she'd ever seen him. That old cowboy hat rested on his head, and he wore a checked, button-up shirt, jeans and she would assume cowboy boots on the feet she couldn't see below the open tailgate.

"Sure. Thanks."

He smiled, causing a flock of butterflies to take flight in her stomach, and grabbed the other end of the table.

"Seems I'm getting into a habit of helping you load or unload heavy, unwieldy furniture."

"You have remarkably good timing." She hopped down from the truck and took the other end of the table. "So I see you changed your mind about com-ing to the rodeo."

"Yeah. Seems I got recruited to ride pickup to-night."

"You're riding in the rodeo?"

"Not in an event. Just helping out, making sure the riders and the animals stay safe."

"Have you done that before?"

"Some, when I was high school. Been a long time."

"But you must have been good or you wouldn't have been asked."

"Decent."

She had a feeling he was downplaying his ability. Rodeo was seriously dangerous, and she'd seen the guys who helped the riders dismount safely and steered bulls and bucking horses out of the arena and away from riders on the ground. It wasn't something just anyone could do.

With a nod, she indicated where she wanted the table to go. When they had it sitting at an angle in her booth area, Austin straightened, took a step back and looked at the table.

"So this is what you do."

"Yep." She couldn't explain the nervous feeling in the pit of her stomach, how she really wanted him to understand her vision.

"What's the story?"

She knew what he was asking. "The door came from an old school way out on the western edge of the county. The rims are from the junkyard. I have about ten bucks in it, including the paint, which I got from a salvage place in San Antonio." Ella reached into her back pocket for the price tags and handed him the appropriate one. "Here, put this on it."

Austin took the tag, his eyes widening when he glanced at it. "People will pay this?"

She shrugged. "We'll find out."

Over the next few minutes, Austin helped her unload the rest of her products as if it was the most natural thing in the world. It felt as easy as their shared lunches had been. Something about that fact made her sad. How fair was it that when she found a guy she liked, to whom she was really attracted, he wasn't someone with whom there could be any sort of future, even if it was casually dating? A part of her almost wished she'd never met him, that the feelings he'd awakened had stayed buried beneath her professional drive.

But she had met him, and she admitted she was dreading the day when he would leave for Dallas and not come back.

"I better get over to the arena," he said.

"Thanks for your help. I was running a bit behind schedule."

"No problem. I can help you load afterward."

It was such a simple thing to say, but a thrill went through her at the idea that they'd be sharing at least a little more time together later.

She knew anyone could see her openly staring at him as he walked toward the chutes behind the arena, where all the riders were gathered, but she couldn't pull her gaze away. If he was leaving in a few days, she was going to look her fill while she had the chance.

"Excuse me," a woman said, drawing Ella's attention.

By the time she'd finished selling the woman a couple of lamps with shades covered in vintage postcards, she could no longer spot Austin in the crowd.

She struggled with distraction throughout the rodeo events. She truly was thankful that lots of customers came through her booth, a healthy number of them making purchases. But she was just as glad when she had a break and she could sit on her tailgate and watch Austin riding around the arena, looking as if he was born in the saddle. If he rode that well after so many years of not doing so, what must he have been like when he did it all the time?

"Careful or your eyeballs might pop out."

Ella jumped at the nearness of the voice beside her, which revealed itself to belong to Keri, who stood next to the truck with her sister-in-law Brooke.

The two women chuckled at her reaction.

"You're right," Brooke said to Keri. "I think she does have it bad."

"What?" Ella realized her mistake the moment she heard how her voice went up. And when Keri and Brooke laughed even harder.

Keri wrapped her arm around Ella's shoulders and looked out toward the arena. "No woman with eyes could blame you for staring. The man is definitely stare-worthy. He was cute in high school, but the years since have been extra kind."

"Careful, you're a married woman," Brooke said, teasing.

Keri looked at her sister-in-law. "Don't stand there and tell me you don't agree with me."

"I plead the Fifth."

Ella sighed. "It's just looking."

"See, you saying that tells me it's more."

"Can't be."

"Why not?"

Ella moved away from Keri and rearranged a few of her displayed items, hoping to get a few more sales now that the last event, the bull riding, was over. "Oh, let me count the reasons." She held up one finger. "We barely know each other." Another finger went up.

"I'm pretty sure he thinks my career is crazy. And, oh yeah, he lives four hours from here. That sort of puts a crimp in any possibility of dating. And the fact he's expressed no interest whatsoever."

Unless that look when they'd been stringing the new fence had meant what her instinct said it had, or at least what something inside her wanted it to. One-way attraction was never fun.

"But you're interested."

Ella threw up her hands. "I'd have to be blind not to be. Hell, I see cowboys every day and haven't thought they were the sexiest thing on two legs. Damn." Her frustration bubbled over. "I don't need this. I have too much on my plate already."

She glanced up just as Keri straightened and looked past her.

"Hey, Austin," Keri said.

Ella froze. Had he heard what she said? Heat surged up her neck to her cheeks, and she didn't think she could face him. She'd probably just killed her chance of getting her hands on the rest of the items in his grandparents' house. She cursed in her head, loud and colorful.

"Keri," he said in that sexy rumble of his. "Long time, no see." When he gave Keri a hug, a rush of jealousy hit Ella like a sudden gust of wind.

"It has been a long time. We should get together soon, catch up, but right now I've got to go get my kiddo from her grandma Merline."

Ella stopped freaking out momentarily to appreciate how sweet it was that Keri's little orphaned niece had been welcomed into the Teague family with open arms. She didn't think Merline and Hank Teague could love that precious little girl any more if she were their own flesh and blood.

But when she sensed Austin move behind her, Ella went right back to freaking out. What should she do? Settling on pretending she hadn't said anything remotely embarrassing, she moved to start loading the items she hadn't sold.

"Someone bought the table?"

The surprise in Austin's voice eased Ella's anxiety some. Either he hadn't heard her or he was choosing the same route as she was of ignoring it and pretending it hadn't happened.

"Yeah, which is nice since we don't have to load it. Actually, I can manage everything that's left if you want to go ahead. You're probably tired."

Instead of leaving, however, he bent to pick up a small table made from an old milk can topped by a round piece of glass covered in pink-and-white lace. He lifted it over the side of her truck bed as if it weighed next to nothing.

Ella had a really ill-timed image of him picking her up that easily.

"I'd venture a guess I'm no more tired than you," he said as he turned to retrieve more of her work.

She couldn't argue with that, and she honestly felt too shaky to say much of anything. Instead, she simply started loading items, too. It took a lot less time than unloading and staging everything, thank goodness, because she wanted nothing more than to go home and hide her face in a pillow. Maybe she'd text Austin in the morning that she was sorry, but she had no more room for anything and he could just hire someone to haul everything else off.

Okay, that was going too far. Wastefulness was one of her biggest pet peeves. She just needed to keep on pretending she hadn't confessed her feelings out loud and hope he hadn't heard her.

When she put the last item in the back of the truck and closed the tailgate, she hazarded a quick glance at Austin. "Thanks for your help. See you tomorrow."

She started to move toward the driver's side door.

"You hungry?"

Though she was in fact starving, having not had time to eat dinner, she lied in answer. "No."

She made the mistake of looking across to where Austin stood on the other side of the truck bed, his forearms propped on the edge. Her stomach flipped. Had he heard what she said and was interested right back? Or was she just imagining she saw something in the way he was looking at her, something other than very early friendship?

Realizing how abrupt her answer had been, she said, "It's been a long day. Just going to hit the hay."

Not giving herself time to change her mind and give in to temptation, Ella opened her door and slipped inside the truck. Without looking back, she started the engine and drove away from the fairgrounds.

MAYBE HE HADN'T heard what he thought he had. Ella had been quick to nix the idea of getting a late dinner after the rodeo the night before, and when he'd arrived at the ranch this morning she'd already been hard at work and threw no more than a quick hello and a wave his way. When she didn't stop for lunch, he debated with himself why. It could just be that she saw the amount of work she had to do before the end of the week, or she was avoiding him. If it was the latter, was it because he'd heard her correctly when she'd been speaking to Keri and was now embarrassed?

Annoyance welled up inside him, and he wasn't entirely sure if it was at Ella for ignoring him or at himself for not wanting her to. It was as if since coming back to Blue Falls, he'd misplaced his brain, forgotten this wasn't his real life.

Hoping a ride would clear his head, he saddled up Duke and rode away from the house and barn. After he'd been riding for a few minutes, he spotted the first of the herd grazing. He edged his way around them, unable to prevent himself from thinking about how Ella had talked to them as if they were overgrown pets. He found himself smiling at the memory, even though that line of thinking didn't have a place on a working ranch. Cattle were raised to make a living for ranching families, not to be giant puppies with names.

He reined in a few minutes later and stared out across the dips and rises in the land. The ranch wasn't the biggest or the best in the area, but it was home. At least out here it felt like it. He'd traveled quite a bit since leaving Blue Falls, but there was no slice of earth or sky that felt quite as right as this. He couldn't deny that an ache accompanied each thought about selling it. But he was also a practical man, and selling it was the practical move. Who kept a place when he could barely stand to step inside the house? When he lived more than two hundred miles away?

He rubbed Duke's neck. "What am I going to do, boy? That woman has me twisted up in knots. And being back here..." He wasn't sure how he really felt about that. Some things brought back happy memories, others not so much.

His phone rang, seeming as out of place here as a doughnut on Mars. After he settled Duke, who'd startled at the noise, a quick glance at the screen showed it was work. No surprise there. What was a surprise was the identity of the person on the other end of the call—not his assistant, Miranda, or even another person in his department but the big boss himself, Frank Lealand. Austin blew out a breath before answering.

"Mr. Lealand, what can I do for you?"

"Your secretary tells me you don't intend to come back to work for another week."

"That's right. I'm settling my grandfather's estate."

"You'll have to put that on hold," Lealand said. "I need you here for a meeting on Friday. All the department heads are required to be there."

Austin had always admired Frank Lealand, even if he was rough around the edges. He'd grown up dirt-poor in nowhere West Texas, went to work in the oil fields when he was just a teenager and built his company from the ground up. But today, his abruptness and seeming lack of feeling rubbed Austin the wrong way. But what could he do about it, tell the old guy off and lose his job? Not after he'd worked hard to pull himself up the corporate ladder.

"Okay." It was all he could manage without letting irritation seep into his voice.

"Good. See you then." Lealand hung up just as abruptly as he did everything else.

Austin resisted the urge to pitch the phone into

the midst of the herd and let them crush it with their hooves. And then realized that only a few days ago the call might not have bothered him so much. He worked hard, did everything that was expected of him and more. He wasn't a pushover, but he didn't ask for anything he didn't believe he deserved either. But the longer he thought about how he was being summoned while out on leave to which he was entitled, the more it irritated him.

He'd just have to work faster to get done before he had to leave and hope he didn't have to make an extra trip back here. When he started to think about how he'd miss seeing Ella every day, he brutally shoved that thought away. He didn't have the luxury of thinking like that. In fact, he was probably going to throw a serious monkey wrench in her plans by telling her she had even less time to clear out the house and buildings. Well, she'd just have to get some help. He certainly didn't have time to help her.

With no time to waste on horseback rides, he turned Duke back toward the house just as he heard thunder in the distance.

The storm overtook him well before he got back to the barn. After taking care of Duke, Austin walked toward the entrance to the barn. Through the pouring rain, he saw movement between him and the house. He squinted and realized it was Ella up in the back of her truck attempting to cover her load with a tarp that kept trying to blow away in the wind.

A flash of lightning was quickly followed by a loud boom of thunder that had Duke shifting in his stall.

"Easy, boy, you're okay in here." Which was more

than Austin could say for Ella. Damn fool woman was
going to get herself electrocuted or break her neck
when she slipped and fell off the truck.

Bracing himself for the onslaught of rain, he raced
toward her pickup.

"Get down from there," he yelled up at her.

She glanced at him. "I need to get this covered."

"Leave it."

She ignored him, making him swear as he grabbed
the edge of the tarp nearest him. The quicker they
got this thing secured, the quicker he could get her to
safety. He hurried to run the rope through the eyelets
with Ella pulling it across the top to the other side. By
the time they had everything under cover, he didn't
think he'd ever been as wet in his life. He reached the
back of the truck as Ella started to get down out of
the bed. Austin didn't give her time, instead grabbing
her around the waist and lifting her to the ground.

His grip slipped on the sopping-wet fabric of her
shirt, and she ended up sliding down the front of his
body. Despite the rain, his body heated and jumped
to full attention. Damn, she felt even better than he'd
imagined in any of his daydreams. Their gazes met,
and her eyes were wider than normal. When her lips
parted, he leaned toward her, unable to stop himself
despite all the reasons this was a bad idea.

Austin let his hand slide along her cheek and to
the back of her head, tilting her at just the right angle.
When his lips captured hers, there was a moment of
hesitation before she kissed him back.

A boom and bright flash caused them both to jump
and break the kiss. It took him a moment to remember why he'd helped her out of the truck in the first

place. He grabbed her hand and ran toward the front steps of the house. Maybe they could continue where they'd left off once they were under a roof.

But when they reached the porch, Ella's wet hand slipped from his and she took a couple of steps away from him.

"Thanks again for your help," she said without looking at him.

Thanks for his help? That's what she had to say after she'd kissed him like that, however brief it might have been? He just stared at her, not having a clue what to say. First she'd told Keri she thought he was sexy, and then she'd given further evidence by kissing him back with what at least felt like enthusiasm. And now she was pretending as though neither had happened? No wonder men complained that they'd never figure out women.

It irritated him enough that he decided to just dump the new deadline on her.

"I've got to be back in Dallas earlier than I thought, so everything will need to be done by midday Thursday."

That actually made her glance at him. After a moment, she nodded. "Understood."

Before he could begin to figure out the tone of her voice, she hurried into the house.

Despite his earlier irritation with his boss, he decided it was a good thing he was headed back to Dallas early, back to things that were tidy and made sense. Away from how being near Ella Garcia short-circuited his brain.

Even though the rain hadn't slackened, he headed down the steps and stalked through the downpour toward his grandfather's truck. When the rain stopped, he planned to have everything he needed to start painting this house right out of his life.

Chapter Eight

Ella stood in the middle of the living room, surrounded by the accumulation of two lifetimes, dripping water on the floor. What had she just done? If she'd only held her attraction in check a few more days, Austin would have been gone. It seemed as if the heavens above had even voiced how it was a bad idea.

Now she faced the final few days of work here on the ranch being incredibly awkward. Because she couldn't let that kiss be repeated. If she did, she suspected she was going to lose her tenuous grip on her feelings and fall for him. And then it would hurt all the more when he left.

Damn it, why had she allowed herself to get to know him, form a friendship behind which she was hiding how much she really liked Austin? If she'd only gotten that tarp on sooner instead of trying to cram a few more things into the truck.

But it was as if she heard a giant ticking clock in her head, and with his revelation on the porch just now the ticking grew louder.

She pushed her dripping hair out of her face and was suddenly overwhelmed by...everything. How much work she still had to do here, not to mention her actual work at home. The tighter deadline for completion. And feelings for Austin that were inconvenient at best. She knew all too well how much it hurt when you loved and lost, so she could not let her feelings for Austin grow anymore. She needed to be cordial, professional, pretend that the lapse in judgment that had just happened hadn't.

If she was going to become involved with someone, it was going to be someone who'd be sticking around, a man who understood and supported her chosen profession. Not someone whose support was limited to helping her load and unload heavy objects.

That was all good in theory, but how was she supposed to forget that kiss? It might have been brief and unexpected, but it had rocked her right off her axis. She'd swear that every nerve ending in her body had sizzled, and she'd never in her life felt such a desire to melt into another human being.

She forced herself to walk into the kitchen and start packing dishes in boxes she'd found in the attic that had mercifully been empty and free for her use. She had to get her mind off Austin, and judging by the sound of an engine outside he must have had the same idea.

As the sound of his grandfather's truck faded beyond the pounding of the rain on the roof, Ella sank onto a chair at the kitchen table. With Austin safely away from the ranch, she allowed herself a moment to admit, if only to herself, that she had loved every second of that kiss and wished it could have gone on forever.

THE WINDSHIELD WIPERS on the old pickup truck couldn't keep up with the downpour, so Austin pulled over at the first spot he could see well enough to do so. His mind was so rattled that he might get washed away in a flash flood before he even realized it.

He turned off the engine and sat listening to the rain beating against the metal above his head. Trying to not think about Ella, he instead focused on the familiar confines of the truck cab. He might be getting rid of the ranch, but maybe he'd keep the truck. He could fix it up and take it out for drives on the weekends.

He leaned his head back and closed his eyes, letting his mind float through scenes from his past that were attached to this vehicle. Riding to town between his grandparents when he'd been barely old enough to see over the dashboard. Sitting on the tailgate eating a sandwich with his grandfather as the older man taught him about running a ranch. Going on his first date, which included dinner in Fredericksburg and then some kissing down by the lake.

That last memory brought his thoughts right back to Ella. Why had he gotten so upset when she'd pulled away? It wasn't as if they were dating. Despite her returning the kiss, maybe he'd caught her off guard. Or misread the level of her interest, not heard her correctly the night before.

Why was he even sitting on the side of the road dissecting what had happened?

Because he liked her, more than anyone he'd dated in a long time. Sure, he didn't really understand her drive to repurpose old stuff, but he wasn't blind to the fact that others appreciated it. The amount of product she'd sold during the rodeo market had shown him that.

Ella was driven, hardworking, friendly—all qualities he admired and respected. He realized that he hadn't had as much fun or been as relaxed in recent memory as he had been sitting on that quilt, eating their lunches together. And soon after she'd met him, she'd seen something he'd thought he'd left behind—the rancher he'd once been. It was as if she'd awakened parts of him that he'd thought dead and buried. As he sat staring at the water coursing down the windshield, he couldn't decide if that was a good or bad thing.

But a voice inside him whispered that it was worth exploring.

His practical side warred with that voice. How could it make sense to start something with Ella when her life was so obviously here and his wasn't anymore? His chance at following in his grandfather's footsteps had long since passed him by.

Not to mention getting involved with her knowing he was leaving in a handful of days wasn't fair to Ella. Everything pointed toward her being a good person, one who deserved more than a long-distance relationship that could never be more.

Austin was surprised by how much his chest ached at the acceptance of what he had to do—imitate Ella and pretend the kiss hadn't happened.

When the rain slackened enough that he could see the road, he started the truck again and drove the rest of the way into town. He parked on the side of Main Street opposite the old-fashioned hardware store. As he sat staring out his window, he wondered if he should have gone somewhere else, even if it would require a drive to another town. With everything else on his mind, he hadn't thought about the fact that he would have to walk across the spot where his grandfather had died.

Yet another reason to return to Dallas as soon as possible. There he wouldn't constantly run into things, people and places that reminded him of what he'd lost.

With a long exhale, he got out of the truck and crossed the street. He didn't slow down until he stepped over the threshold of the hardware store. As he had the first day he'd gone into the Primrose Café after returning to Blue Falls, he received a lot of condolences from the other patrons who recognized him. He could tell from the look in some people's eyes that they had made the connection between where he was and where his grandfather had breathed his last breath.

He made his way down one of the aisles to the paint section and started looking at color samples. How many different shades of white could there be? As he read some of the names, he wondered just whose job it was to sit around and come up with those.

"Can I help you find something?"

He glanced over to see a young man, looking eager to dispense some friendly, small-town customer service.

"I'd like some paint the color of limestone."

As if the guy got that exact question all the time, he reached for a color card. "Will this work?"

"I guess. I can't tell the difference in over half of these."

The young man laughed. "It takes some getting used to."

Austin set the guy to mixing enough paint to cover

the necessary square footage. While waiting for that, Austin started tossing other supplies in a small cart.

The sound of giggling drew his attention to the opposite end of the aisle, where a man and woman were all smiles as they appeared to tease each other. Something shifted inside Austin, unveiling a feeling of being so alone that was strong enough it almost knocked him down.

Despite all the reasons he knew it was a terrible idea, he wanted more with Ella. It might not go anywhere, but damn if he didn't want to see for sure. They could keep it casual, just some fun for two hardworking, stressed-out people. They deserved that, right? He wished he hadn't driven away in a huff. Instead, he should have tried to talk to her. Isn't that what women always wanted, to talk about their feelings?

He shook his head. What was wrong with him? He wasn't looking for a long-distance relationship, no matter how casual. And in a handful of days, that's exactly what anything with Ella would be.

He tossed a roller tray and plastic to cover the windows into the cart and headed back to the paint counter. After picking up the paint, he pointed his cart toward the cashier. A couple of people were ahead of him, and his gaze wandered to the various event posters tacked to the front of the wooden counter. Looked like the area was hosting everything from a car show and barbecue to a pie and cake auction at the Blue Falls Music Hall to benefit the local high school's rodeo team. Something about all those posters made him smile. They felt comfortable, as if they were just different venues at which friends and neighbors could hang out because they liked each other. He went to plenty of events in Dallas, many enjoyable, but they didn't have the "home" feeling these did.

After paying for his supplies, he stepped out the front door but stopped on the single low step between the door and the sidewalk. Where exactly had his grandfather fallen? No, he didn't want to know.

"It was right there."

He jerked his attention toward the voice, recognizing it even before he saw Ella standing there, still damp from the rain.

"What?"

"The day your grandfather passed, I was here. I... saw the paramedics working with him. I only heard later that he hadn't made it."

He looked back at the spot a bit to the left of the entryway she'd indicated.

"I really am sorry. He always seemed like a nice man."

He nodded. "He was." A lump grew in his throat. He'd been avoiding thinking about the loss by focusing instead on all the work that loss had caused. After a few moments, he returned his gaze to Ella. "Why are you here?"

"Can we talk?"

Not knowing how the conversation would go, he still found himself nodding. Clearing the air was a good thing, much better than tiptoeing around each other for the next few days or her disappearing and him having to find someone else to clear out the ranch buildings, most likely someone who would charge and wouldn't be able to get to it immediately.

After he dropped off his supplies at the truck, he walked beside her as they headed down Main Street.

Despite her saying she wanted to talk, she stayed quiet. And oddly he didn't mind. When they reached the end of the connected buildings, Ella took the path that led down to the lake. When she reached the lake's edge, she stopped.

"I'm sorry I reacted the way I did earlier," she said. "You just caught me by surprise."

He stood looking at her profile for a moment, surprised by her words. He'd expected that maybe she was angry, offended, something that wouldn't end in an apology from her. One that wasn't warranted.

"You have nothing to apologize for. I should be the one to do that. I'm sorry."

As she turned her head toward him, there was a little smile on her face. "Or maybe neither of us has to apologize?"

He wasn't particularly good at reading women, not that any guy he knew was. "And that means?"

Ella glanced away toward the lake stretching out in front of them, a few fishing boats and a couple of sailboats dotting the surface. "That perhaps we both enjoyed it, and maybe that's not a bad thing."

Austin's pulse kicked it up a couple of notches. "I'm not staying, Ella."

"I know."

"And you're okay with that?"

"Would I be here if I wasn't?"

He wasn't totally sure he believed her, but he was damn tired of resisting the attraction between them that had started pretty much from the day they'd met.

"Okay." He shifted to face her fully. "Tomorrow, we knock off work early and do something fun."

"We don't have much time left to finish the work at the ranch."

"Then we work extra hard during the day."

She looked up at him with those large, dark brown eyes of hers. "Okay. What will we do?"

He knew what he wanted to do, but despite her assertion that she was okay with just a few days together, he didn't think she meant that. "I'll think of something."

"Either you're a man of mystery or clueless."

He smiled. "I'll let you guess which one."

She laughed at that, and the sound made the heaviness inside him lighten. Ella had that incredible ability, to make him feel like the world was somehow brighter when she was around. Damn, that was cheesy, but the truth was the truth. Yes, there were differences between them and she could be frustrating, but he was sure he wasn't a peach to deal with at times either.

"Well, then," she said. "I better get back to work. And you have a house to paint."

For the briefest moment, he thought she was forcing herself to look chipper, but then whatever had made him think that was gone.

"Hopefully I'm better with painting supplies than gutters."

She smiled again, and he thought he'd never seen a more beautiful woman. "Yeah, I'd hate to show up tomorrow to find you flat on the ground with a paint bucket on your head."

He wanted to pull her close and kiss her before she left, but he didn't know how she'd feel about that. Sure, she'd sought him out to basically say she liked kissing him and wouldn't mind doing it again, but would she feel the same if he laid one on her in public, especially in Blue Falls, where it could quite possibly be front-page news?

He might not have touched her before she turned and started retracing her steps toward the street, but he certainly enjoyed the view. And anyone who happened to be watching him would know in a microsecond that he wanted nothing more than to touch Ella.

How in the world was he going to concentrate on work until tomorrow night?

UNABLE TO SLEEP despite being beyond tired, Ella was at the ranch at sunrise the next morning. Before she got to work, she took a few moments to watch the sun's rays stretch out across the land. She loved this time of day when everything seemed filled with endless possibilities.

And maybe today was. Somehow she had to get through a long day of work to find out what Austin had planned for their...date. It seemed weird to even think of it that way. She'd gone on a date here and there, but never with someone who caused her blood to run the Kentucky Derby through her veins.

Part of her mind kept whispering that this was a really bad idea. Why would she put herself in a situation where she might grow to like him even more when she knew he was leaving Blue Falls for good?

Because she was tired of being alone. She knew she couldn't, but she wanted to hate him for making her realize that when she thought she was going along just fine on her own. Only she'd simply been hiding behind nonstop work without realizing it. She wondered if she'd been doing that since her father died. Then she'd buried herself in school, extracurricular activities, crafts and reading. Now it was her business and working hard to become a part of her community.

She reminded herself that it was her choice to see what they might be able to share in the next few days. Maybe it would be enough to cure the lonely feeling inside her middle and she could go back to the way life had been before sexy Austin Bryant had strolled into it.

ELLA SHOVED AN unruly curl, the one that always seemed to have a mind of its own, behind her ear as she walked to the entrance of La Cantina. As soon as she walked in, she spotted Austin. Damn, did the man ever look anything other than drop-dead gorgeous?

He noticed her and smiled as he crossed the lobby, his hat—a new cream-colored straw one—in hand.

"You look beautiful," he said.

Warmth spread through her body, and it had absolutely nothing to do with the heat outside. Despite the kiss they'd shared, he'd never said anything so complimentary before. The time she'd taken digging through her closet for the lime-green dress and getting ready—for herself as much as Austin—had totally been worth it.

"Thank you. Not looking half-bad yourself, cowboy."

He appeared momentarily surprised, and she wondered if it was because she'd complimented his looks or that she'd called him a cowboy. He might not self-identify that way anymore, but that's how she saw him. And she thought that maybe deep down he did, too. It was just hard to admit because it brought him closer to a past that held some sad memories.

"I hope this place is okay." He looked so nervous all of a sudden that she couldn't help but chuckle.

"You mean because I'm part Hispanic and we're at the only Mexican place in town? Oh, honey, I haven't met a tortilla I didn't like. Get me near a Taco Cabana, and I can do some serious damage."

"Good."

He looked so relieved she just had to tease him. "But if there is a sombrero anywhere in my immediate future, I'm outta here."

This time he chuckled and placed his hand over his heart. "No sombreros, mariachi singers or piñatas."

The hostess came to lead them to their table. Once they were seated, Ella grew nervous, afraid they'd find nothing to talk about. So she immediately picked up her menu to study it even though she already knew what she wanted. When it came to food, she was more often than not a creature of habit. Still, Austin didn't know that, and she used the time she was supposedly reading the menu to try to form a list of possible conversation topics.

"What are you having?" he asked.

"I'm not sure." Chicken chimichanga. "So many good choices."

By the time the waitress took their orders, Ella thought she was going to be sick. Why had she thought this was a good idea?

"So, tell me about your plans for your business."

Ella looked up from the spot on the table she'd been staring a hole through. "What?"

He smiled. "You seem nervous, and I figure your business would be an easy topic for you to talk about."

She relaxed more than she'd thought possible only moments before. "You sure you want to hear about this?"

"Yes. Maybe I can help."

She lifted a brow. "You think what I do is stupid."

"I never said that. I recognize there are a lot of trends I don't understand. Doesn't make them any less profitable."

"It's not all about the money."

"You should want it to be about the money."

She sat back on her side of the booth and crossed her arms. "I want to be a success, yes. But I work so hard at this for other reasons. I love the creative outlet, and I hate the idea of our throwaway society and waste."

Austin leaned forward, his forearms on the top of the table. "That's fine. But if you want all your work and passion to result in a profitable career, then you have to have a business plan. Know what you want and how to get there."

She mentally flipped through all the ideas she'd had about her business and decided to just tell him about her biggest dreams. If he thought they were crazy, well, he'd be gone soon and it wouldn't matter.

"I want my own storefront and a thriving Internet business, to eventually be successful enough that I can hire people to handle all the business stuff so I can work on the creative side. To grow enough that I can bring on more designers who feel the way I do about making beautiful pieces out of things that would normally be thrown away."

"Okay, big goals. That's good. What have you done to move toward those?"

"I have a website, and I get jobs via word of mouth."

"And?"

"Um, I have a whole lot of raw materials to work with." She gave him a tentative smile.

"So more acquisitions than sales?"

She sighed. "Yes."

Austin held up a hand. "Not a criticism. Just have to have the whole picture in order to help."

As they waited for their meals, she took him through her finished-stock situation, storage, capital outlay, raw materials, sales and several other aspects of her business. She handed over the thin laptop she always had with her, and he scanned her numbers.

She nervously munched on chips and guacamole as he flipped through her pages of documentation. This was like no date she'd ever been on, but excitement filled her nonetheless. That and no small amount of anxiety. She'd never shared this much about her business with anyone, and the fact that Austin had a business degree and worked at a large company made her hope to gain some valuable insight into making her business what she envisioned. Of course, the longer he looked at her laptop, the more her insides twisted that he would think it all an unholy mess. It was a testament to how hungry she was that she could even eat the chips.

"My first suggestion is that after you finish with the ranch, you concentrate on preparing things to sell. One, you'll increase your revenue. And you won't become so overwhelmed with things you have to store."

She detected the hint of disdain, not toward her personally but the idea of too much stuff in too small a space. That, combined with the fact he'd been in his grandparents' house only once—and only briefly then—since she'd met him, made her wonder something.

"Are you claustrophobic?"

He looked up from her computer just as the waitress arrived with their food. They didn't speak other than to say thank you to the waitress until she was gone.

"That would explain a lot," she said.

At first she thought he was going to deny it, probably didn't like admitting that weakness.

"Yes."

She nodded then shifted her gaze to her computer. "What else?"

He didn't immediately reply, as if he'd thought she was going to make a big deal out of the claustrophobia.

"Everyone's scared of something," she said. "Me, it's snakes. I don't care if they're poisonous or not, big as an anaconda or small as an earthworm, if I see one I'm probably going to scream like that blonde chick in *Temple of Doom*."

Austin smiled, making her insides tingle.

"Way to pull out the old reference."

"My dad loved Indiana Jones. We watched those movies over and over when I was growing up. Now, you were about to tell me how I can become a fabulously wealthy designer."

As they ate, Austin went into full-on businessman mode. The fact that he still looked like a cowboy while doing it, showing his brain was just as sexy as the rest of him, made her want to drag him home and straight to bed. She wasn't normally the hop-into-bed sort of person, but she felt as if she'd been waiting to do exactly that from the moment she'd met him. The magnetic pull toward him wasn't like anything she'd ever experienced.

"What do you think?" he asked.

Oh, crap. She'd missed whatever he'd been saying while fantasizing about him. "Huh?"

He closed the laptop. "I'm sorry. I've made this more like a business meeting than a date."

She reached across the table and placed her hand over his. "Honestly, this is the best date I've been on in forever."

"So you haven't been on a date in the last decade?"

She playfully swatted his hand. "No, seriously. I don't really have an opportunity to talk to anyone about my dreams for the business. It's nice, and energizing."

"What about your mom?"

She started to pull her hand away, but he didn't let her, instead entwining his fingers with hers. Her heart beat extra hard at the gesture before she remembered Austin had asked her a question.

"I can talk to her about it some, and she likes what I make. It's just that…she's seen how easy it is to fail at something, and I think she worries."

"Because of your stepfather?"

"Yeah. I mean, he's a decent enough guy. He just doesn't have much of a head for business but thinks he does. I tried to explain to her that I'm different, that I love what I do, that I will do whatever it takes to make it a success. He easily jumps into ventures other people tell him are a surefire thing."

"And they never are."

"Right again. Then he'll work in a regular job for a while until the next can't-miss opportunity comes along, and the cycle begins again. I feel bad for my mom sometimes. I'm not even sure she really loves Jerry. She just happened to meet him a few months after my dad died, and they got married a couple of weeks later. I think she was scared of being alone, or raising me alone. But it took me a long time to forgive her for that. At the time, it felt as if she was replacing my dad like he was a car that had quit running. I was angry for years."

"What finally healed the relationship?"

"I walked in on her once holding a photo of my dad in uniform, and she was crying. I mean ugly, my-soul-is-broken crying. And just like that, my anger dissolved. It was the oddest, most freeing feeling. I sat down beside her on the bed, and we held each other for a long time." Tears welled in Ella's eyes at the memory, as they always did when she thought about it.

Austin squeezed her hand, then pulled his away to retrieve his wallet and toss enough money on the table for the check and tip. Then he took her hand again.

"Come on. No more business or sad stories. Time to have some fun."

Chapter Nine

When they stepped outside, instead of heading toward their vehicles, Austin led Ella down the sidewalk in the opposite direction.

"What's your favorite flavor of dessert?" he asked.

She pointed behind them. "You realize we just left the restaurant, right? And the bakery is in the opposite direction."

He just looked over at her, expectation and quite possibly a bit of mischief in his eyes.

"Strawberry. Why?"

"Just so happens there is a pie and cake auction at the music hall tonight."

"To benefit the high school rodeo team. I've seen the posters."

"I figured maybe dessert and music might make up for talking business all through dinner."

"I told you I didn't mind. My head's already buzzing with ideas based on what you said."

He didn't look convinced he hadn't been the biggest dud of a date ever, and she had the wicked notion of showing him later just how much he wasn't a dud. Her cheeks flushed, but thankfully she could blame that on the heat as they crossed the parking lot to the music hall.

As they walked in, the Teagues of Texas—brothers Simon, Nathan and Ryan Teague—were just launching into a Willie Nelson tune on stage, always popular with the local crowd.

Austin still held her hand as he maneuvered them from the corner entrance through the crowd toward the front wall. Some of the tables had been pushed against the length of the wall and were laden with cakes and pies of every imaginable kind.

"I think I felt three cavities form just looking at this," she said.

Austin laughed. "Come on, let's see which ones are strawberry."

"We don't need an entire cake or pie."

"Sure we do."

As they examined the offerings, Ella soaked up the feel of his hand wrapped around her smaller one. She couldn't remember the last time a guy had held her hand. To her, it felt more important than kissing. She had to remind herself not to read too much into it. They were just going to have a few days of fun, then they'd go back to their respective lives and likely other people.

"This looks good." Austin pointed to a five-layer cake covered in cream cheese frosting and an abundance of strawberries. "Says it has strawberries between every layer, too." He indicated the written description on the tented card beside it.

Her mouth watered, but then she spotted something else a little farther down the line. She urged Austin in that direction. She read the card as she tried not to melt from Austin's nearness behind her.

"Just as I thought," she said. "Keri made these. They are to die for. She puts some sort of secret ingredient in them that makes them—" She almost said "orgasmic," but even thinking that was dangerous right now, like it might become a self-fulfilling prophecy. "Delicious."

"Hey, you two." The voice that sent single people who wanted to stay single fleeing.

Ella turned, casually taking a step away from Austin. She did not want to give the other woman the wrong idea. She and Austin were temporary at best.

"Hey, Verona. Which dessert do you have your eye on?"

"What I have my eye on is you two. I knew you'd make a cute couple."

"We're not a couple."

Verona grinned in her knowing way. "Maybe not yet, but you're off to a good start. I hear you spent quite a bit of time at dinner, very involved in conversation."

"About business."

"Uh-huh."

Not that she didn't like the idea of being with Austin, but Ella was approaching whatever they would share realistically. Verona was a nice lady who did a lot for the community, but her penchant for aggressive matchmaking could grate on a person's nerves.

Ella pulled her computer from her purse. "I can show you."

Verona looked genuinely startled. "No, no. Just go and have a good time." She moved quickly past Ella and Austin into the crowd, probably already zeroing in on her next target.

"Is it just me or is she not used to not getting her way?" A grin tugged at the edges of Austin's mouth.

"Don't get too excited," Ella said as she slipped her computer back into her purse. "She's probably just retreating long enough to come up with a new plan of attack. Maybe you'll be able to make your escape before then."

"Yeah."

What was that odd tone in Austin's voice? It almost sounded like regret, but that couldn't be right. Maybe the part of her brain that wished he wasn't leaving was trying to play a cruel trick on her.

But what if…?

"Wanna dance?"

Austin shook his head. "I'm a terrible dancer."

"And yet you brought me to a dance hall."

"It's a music hall, says so on the sign."

"Music meant to be danced to." She grabbed his hand. "Come on. Let's really confuse Verona."

When he tried to protest again, she just dragged him to the dance floor. "Oh, quit whining. Anybody can dance at least a little bit."

But after a couple of minutes of seeing Austin's attempts, she couldn't hold in the laughter anymore. "Okay, I was wrong. You really can't dance."

"I told you. I think I'll keep dancing just to embarrass you now." He exaggerated his horrible dance moves until she grabbed his arm and pulled him toward the edge of the dance floor.

"You're liable to throw something out of joint, or punch someone in the eye."

"Is that any way to talk to the guy giving you tons of free supplies?"

She stopped once they were off the dance floor and looked up at him. "I'm just saving you from yourself."

"What if I don't want saving?" His voice grew huskier with those words. Before she could say they needed to be careful because Verona was surely watching, along with half of the rest of Blue Falls she'd have to see once Austin was gone, he reached out and started to pull her closer.

Dimly she became aware the music had stopped and someone had started talking into the microphone. She forced herself to shift and look toward the stage. Liam Parrish, who ran the local rodeos and was married to her friend India, turned out to be the speaker.

"We'll get back to the music in a while, but as you know we're here to make some money tonight for the young riders on the Blue Falls High School rodeo team."

A round of cheers went up as Liam pointed toward several teenagers standing beside the stage.

"We've got some delicious-looking cakes and pies here tonight, and I can already tell you I'm going to outbid everyone for my wife's fudge pie."

This time laughter came from the crowd. Ella spotted India over next to the teen riders, looking at her husband as if he were the only man in the room. Something moved deep inside Ella, a yearning to have that kind of connection with someone, to be so obviously loved.

She prevented herself from looking at Austin because she was afraid he'd see what she was thinking and feeling in her expression. It was crazy to even have such thoughts about someone she hadn't known long.

Was she playing with emotional fire by going out with him? Instead of enjoying these few days, was she setting herself up to be hurt, as illogical as that might seem?

Austin leaned toward her. "You okay?"

She nodded. "Yeah. Just curious how much people will be willing to pay for desserts." And how any of those sweet treats would taste on his lips.

AUSTIN COULDN'T FIGURE out if Ella had pulled away because she thought Verona was watching or she was having second thoughts about being out with him on a date. She'd been quick to tell Verona they'd had a working dinner. While part of him thought he understood her reasoning, it had still annoyed him some. And he wasn't even sure it was her he was annoyed at and not himself. This was going nowhere beyond the next few days.

Suddenly, he wanted those few days to be full of Ella, and more than working together at the ranch or sharing a meal in public. He longed to kiss her right now, right here, but he didn't want to chance being smacked.

They watched and cheered with the rest of the crowd as one dessert after another brought nice prices. When they got to the strawberry tarts Ella had praised, he didn't wait for anyone else to bid.

"Two hundred dollars," he called out before the description was even complete.

He heard several gasps, including one from Ella.

"Are you crazy?" she asked in a whisper.

The thought that he could very easily be crazy about her popped into his head.

"So, anyone going to try to beat that?" Liam asked from the stage.

Silence answered him.

"Okay then, strawberry tarts to Austin Bryant."

Austin moved to the stage to claim the tray of tarts, then returned to Ella, who still looked stunned that he had spent so much. She wasn't the only one, but she seemed to have a way of making him act out of character. And he liked it.

"What do you say we go try these out?"

She nodded and led the way toward the exit.

Despite the fact it was still warm outside, it felt better than the stuffy confines of the music hall. Plus, he'd a million times rather be alone with Ella than the object of either curiosity or condolences in the crowd.

"Want to go sit at the park and give these a try?" he asked.

"You know you're crazy, right?"

He shrugged. "There are worse things to be."

They walked the short distance to the park beside the lake. On the hill above it, the lights of the Wildflower Inn shone in the darkness.

Austin placed his hand at the small of Ella's back and guided her toward one of the picnic tables. They sat on the same side, facing the lake. The reflection of the quarter-moon seemed to reach out from the lake toward them.

He pulled the wrapper off the tray of tarts and extended one of the strawberry treats to Ella. As she took it, their fingers grazed each other. Ella's gaze rose to meet his.

"Why did you pay so much for these?"

"I had to get out of there before you made me dance again."

She laughed. "There was zero chance of that."

"Ouch."

Ella smiled then bit into her tart. She made a sound of appreciation that caused everything that made him male snap to attention.

When he took a bite of his own tart, he understood her reaction. "This is good."

"And the award for Understatement of the Year goes to…"

He bumped her shoulder with his own. "You want me to start spouting off poetry about it?"

"That might be interesting." She propped her head on her upturned hand as if she couldn't wait to hear his attempt at being a poet.

"Don't hold your breath."

"Tease. You go and get me all excited for odes to desserts, and then back out."

"How about this instead?" He lowered his lips to hers, cradling her head against his palm.

After a moment of surprise, she kissed him back with her strawberry-flavored lips. He'd meant for it to be a quick kiss, but her reaction fueled his barely banked desire. The truth was he'd been attracted to Ella from that first day. Just looking at her made his temperature rise and his hands itch to hold her, to take her.

Ella placed her hand against his chest and pushed away a little. "I thought we were here to have dessert."

"Tastes pretty good to me."

She laughed a little and smiled up at him. Something about seeing her in the moonlight made her even more beautiful. It was more than just physical attraction, though. He liked her as a person. He admired her work ethic, and she made him laugh and relax. Maybe it was so noticeable because he didn't normally do either enough.

"You can't taunt a gal with a great dessert and not let her finish it."

He leaned back, letting her go. Despite the fact that the tart was really good, all he could think about was tasting Ella again. And the longer he sat and thought about it, the more he wanted to sample more than her lips.

"Really, why did you pay so much for these?" Ella asked as she wiped strawberry topping from the corner of her mouth. "I mean, I'm sure the rodeo team appreciates it, but it's a lot of money."

In truth, he'd done it before he'd thought it through. He knew how it would look to everyone else in the crowd, but in this moment he didn't care.

"You wanted them, and I wanted to get out of that crush of people." He cupped her jaw and ran the pad of his thumb over her lips. "I wanted to be alone with you."

He was treading on dangerous ground here, but he couldn't deny that the pull toward Ella was stronger every time he was around her.

"Oh."

He smiled. "You're not normally a woman of so few words."

"My brain isn't usually this scrambled."

"Is that a good or bad thing?"

Her smile looked nervous, shaky. "Good."

He couldn't keep his hands off her anymore, so he pulled her close to him on the bench and kissed her again, deeper this time and more full of the fire she'd lit inside him. Ella ran her hands up his back and pressed even closer to him.

He moved his mouth to her neck and kissed a trail down to where her breasts swelled at the top of her dress.

"Oh."

Ella's single word, the way she said it as if the mere touch of his lips could bring her to climax, damn near did it to him. She dug her fingers into the muscles of his back, and the next thing he knew she was crawling up on him, her thighs straddling his leg.

"This is crazy," she said in a husky voice before she threaded her hands in his hair, knocking off his hat, and kissed him the way a man liked to be kissed.

She was right. This was crazy, and he liked it. Before he flattened her on the picnic table and took her under the moonlight in a public park, he broke the kiss.

"Come back to my room with me."

"Someone will see us," she said into his ear, sending even more heat surging through his body.

"You're killing me, woman."

The sound of her giggle made him growl and capture her mouth again. When he had to take a breath, he said, "We'll go in the back. Half the town is at the music hall, and the other half is asleep."

The hesitance he felt in her made him pull back and caress her shoulder.

"I…don't know."

He sensed an inner struggle going on, her mind

against the rest of her body. "I won't push, but I also won't lie. I want you, Ella. Bad."

Again, she hesitated. When she finally slid off his leg and stood, he envisioned the ice-cold shower he was going to be forced to take. But then she extended her hand to him, and he couldn't follow her fast enough.

ELLA KEPT SCANNING her surroundings as if she were a burglar trying not to get caught. After telling Verona that she and Austin weren't a couple and considering the fact that he was leaving in a few days, the last thing she wanted was to be caught sneaking to his hotel room.

More than once she considered digging in her heels, stopping this madness before it went past the point of no return. But each time an increasingly loud voice in her head told her to go for it, to capture whatever pleasure and happiness she could when she could because you were never guaranteed another day in this life.

She held on to Austin's hand, trying not to slip in her little sandals. He led her toward the side entrance to the Wildflower Inn, the tray of strawberry tarts in his other hand. When they reached the door, he peeked through the small window.

"Nobody in the hallway," he said, then released her hand to slide his key card through the reader and open the door.

Ella held her breath as he reclaimed her hand and led the way inside. With each step she took, she feared someone she knew would come around a corner and catch her. It would be as obvious as stripes on a zebra why she was there in a hotel with a man holding her hand and leading her toward his room.

She still couldn't believe she was doing this, but excitement and anticipation pumped through her. Why did Austin's room have to be so far from the exit? Was he right next to the flipping lobby?

Finally, he stopped in front of a room halfway down the corridor and again released her hand to unlock the door. Despite the fact that she was anxious to not be seen, she hesitated outside the room. But then she met Austin's beautiful blue eyes and saw hunger in them. It fanned the flames of her own and she stepped into his room.

Despite the desire she felt radiating off him, he slowly slid the tray of tarts onto a small table then walked toward her. He stopped only inches from her.

"Do you want this, Ella?"

Again, she hesitated, but not as long this time. No matter what happened in the days ahead, she wanted this now. Wanted every bit she could share with Austin before reality came crashing back down on top of her.

"Yes."

He lowered his mouth to hers, kissing her slowly, deeply. But the fire burning within her demanded more, faster. She ran her hands up his chest, then started unbuttoning his shirt.

Austin chuckled against her lips. "In a hurry?"

She leaned back just enough to meet his gaze. "Yes."

His expression changed from amused to aroused. In the next moment he captured her mouth again, but this time it was as if he were starving and she was the

only meal for miles. He backed her against the wall
as she finished with the buttons, exposing his flesh
to her questing fingers. The warmth, the texture, the
thumping of his heart made her moan into his mouth.

Austin responded by running his hands underneath
the bottom of her dress. The feel of those male hands,
roughened by recent work on the ranch, was almost
enough to make her climax right there. His lips left
her mouth and traveled downward. This time, however, he didn't stop at the swell of her breast. Instead,
he shoved the cup of her bra aside and took her between those hot, moist lips.

Undiluted pleasure shot through her, causing her
to throw her head back, thumping it into the wall.

"Are you okay?" Austin asked, a concern in his
voice that just made him so much sexier, which didn't
seem possible.

"I will be if you go back to what you were doing."

"With pleasure." Not only did he return to the delicious working of her breast, but he unhooked her bra
and gave the other breast equal attention.

Ella's legs began to shake. In response, Austin
shoved her dress up and over her head. She let her
bra fall to the ground and kicked off her slip-on sandals, leaving only her underwear. He pressed his body
against hers, and it was obvious that he was as turned
on as she was.

The way he caressed her face as he looked down
at her made Ella fall a little more for him. Yeah, she
was falling, she couldn't help it. But she'd deal with
that later. She wanted this man so much she thought
she might burst from it. He seemed to be asking with
his eyes if she was sure. In answer, she shoved his

shirt off his shoulders and ran her tongue slowly up and across one of his nipples.

Austin growled like an animal and spun her away from the wall and up into his arms. He stalked to the bed, then set her on her feet right beside it. Feeding off his hunger, she kissed him again as her hands went to his belt and pulled it free, then lowered the zipper on his jeans. She slipped a hand inside and grazed the hot, hard length of him.

"Stop," Austin hissed between his teeth. "Or this will be over before we even get in that bed."

She liked the feeling of power that came over her. "What do you propose I do instead?"

"How about get rid of these?" He slid his hands beneath the edges of her underwear and started pushing them down her legs.

When she felt them fall around her ankles, she nipped at Austin's lower lip. "Your turn."

He took a step backward and shoved his boots off, then his jeans and underwear. She'd never seen such a beautiful man in her entire life. How were there not women lined up from here to Dallas waiting and hoping to find their way into his arms, into his bed? She couldn't believe she was the one here.

Austin closed the distance between them and urged her back onto the bed. He followed and at the feel of all that skin on skin, it was as if firecrackers started popping all over her body, from where his mouth captured hers to where her toes rubbed against the lower part of his leg.

"You feel good," he said between kisses.

"So do you." But she knew what would feel so

much better. She rubbed her foot up the back of his leg and lifted her body up into his.

Austin froze. "I'm trying to go slow here."

She ran her tongue along the edge of his ear. "What if I don't want to go slow?"

He grabbed her behind her knees and pulled her legs apart. "Then I guess I'll have to give you what you want."

She gasped as he captured her mouth again, devouring her as his hand slid between her legs. Raw need had her pressing up against his hand, her yearning throbbing inside her. He made quick work of readying her, which caused her to whimper when he rolled away. Before she could verbalize a protest, however, he was back and so close to giving her what she wanted.

"Ella—" There was something in his voice, like he might be about to ask her if she really wanted this.

She didn't want to think, didn't want him to either. They were grown-ups, not overwrought teens, and they had grown-up needs. She hoped he understood that when she placed her finger over his lips, stopping him from saying whatever he'd been about to give voice.

"I want you," she said.

That was all it took to send him over the edge. He pushed inside her with a thrust that had her throwing back her head, this time into a blessedly soft pillow instead of the unforgiving wall. But the thought flitted through her mind that it was going to be difficult to keep this quiet, not when she ached to give full volume to the pleasure.

Ella's mind spun and her body reached for fulfillment. Each stroke brought her closer, and from the way Austin's movements were increasing in speed, he was likely on the verge, as well.

"Yes," she breathed into his ear. "Now."

Her breath came in gasps and pants. Austin held her close as he urged them both toward completion. Just…a…little…more.

Ella cried out as she peaked. The pleasure increased as she watched Austin's neck and torso stiffen and him throw his head back with his eyes closed as he climaxed. She had never seen anything more magnificent, more arousing. She knew in that moment that she was in trouble. She was falling in love with Austin Bryant.

Austin collapsed beside Ella, trying to catch his breath. Beside him, Ella lay on her back in a similar state. That had been, no exaggeration, the best sex of her life. Every touch, every stroke, every sound of pleasure had added high-octane fuel to the fire burning within her.

"Well, I don't think that was as quiet as I planned," she said.

Austin barked out a laugh and rolled to face her. "I guess we'll have to find a bag for you to wear over your head when you leave."

He was so attuned to the slightest change in her body now that he felt her stiffen. Did she think he was about to kick her out? Not likely. He didn't want to think about leaving this room anytime soon. He pulled her close and kissed her.

"Thank you," he said between kisses.

Ella ran her hand over his shoulder. "You're thanking me for sex?"

"Yes. I know it's a big deal for women."

She stiffened again. Good grief, he couldn't say anything right. Before she pulled away, he caressed her face.

"That was the best I've ever had."

Austin realized he should probably keep tonight to actions and not words, but something deep inside him felt right telling her, even if this ended up being the only night they spent together. But he hoped it wasn't. He had a few more before he left, and he couldn't think of a better way to spend them than in bed with Ella.

She curled up close, her cheek against his chest. "Me, too."

Two of the simplest words in the world, but they sent a surge of pride and happiness through him that was so potent it made him want to beat his chest like a gorilla. He placed a kiss atop her head and pulled the comforter over them. He wasn't letting her go until he had to.

Chapter Ten

Ella woke disoriented. The bed didn't feel right—too soft. The feel of warm, male skin pressed along her back, bottom and legs brought a rush of hot memories back.

Austin. The most awesome sex imaginable. She replayed it in her mind, the result being she wanted a repeat performance. A glance at the clock revealed it was a little after two in the morning. She needed to make her way back to her truck while it was less likely she'd be seen, but she just couldn't move yet. If she left, she might never be able to experience this with Austin again. Though she knew she should leave before she fell any harder, instead she rolled toward him.

Feeling more daring in the darkened room, she kissed the curve of his jaw, ran her hand slowly down his chest and across the flat expanse of his stomach. He stirred and mumbled, "What are you doing?"

"I'd think that was obvious," she said, feeling quite unlike herself. "Seducing you."

She'd never seduced a man, never made the first move, and she had to admit it was intoxicating. Though chances were good she'd die of embarrassment when she had to face him in the light of day. But she'd deal with that when the time came.

Ella crawled atop Austin, placing a leg on each side of his hips. His body sprang to attention as his eyes widened. She guided him inside her and set the pace, starting slow and sensuous.

Austin grasped her bottom and rose to meet her gliding movements.

"Damn, you're beautiful."

Her heart filled with joy. It wasn't wise and she'd pay for it later, but she was pretty sure she loved this man. To keep from thinking about losing him, she increased the pace. When Austin lifted his upper half and captured one of her breasts in his mouth, she was lost.

A few minutes later, after they'd both gotten their breathing back under control, she said the words she'd been putting off. "I need to go."

"It's the middle of the night."

"And thus the best time for me to get out undetected." And if she spent the entire night with Austin, it would feel more like a relationship, which it wasn't. This was no more than two people satisfying physical needs.

Okay, it was more for her, but she couldn't say that. He'd freak out, and giving her feelings voice would just make them more real, harder to deal with when Austin put Blue Falls and her in his rearview mirror.

He started to pull her closer, but she eased away.

"As much as I'd like to stay longer, one of us has to stay here and face the locals," she said. "If Verona hears about this, I will have to become a hermit who never answers the front door."

She slipped from the bed, and was glad the dim lighting hid how her skin flushed at the idea of him watching her naked body as she retrieved her clothes. She didn't make eye contact as she dressed, and breathed more easily only when she heard him slip out of the bed and start dressing, as well.

When she had everything back on, she turned and found him fully clothed. "You don't have to come with me."

"I'm not letting you walk back to your truck alone."

"It's Blue Falls. I'll be fine."

"Bad things happen everywhere." He reached out his hand, making it clear there was no use arguing with him.

She took his hand, wondering if she'd still be thinking about the feel of his fingers entwined with hers years from now.

He checked the hallway and nodded that the coast was clear. She fought the urge to giggle, like she was being naughty and getting away with it.

Then the exterior door started to open, and before she could fully panic, Austin pulled her into the vending area. He ushered her to the opposite side of the ice machine at the far end of the small room, which should hide them from whoever was out there unless they decided they needed a wee-hours bucket of ice.

Ella held her breath as the footsteps grew closer. She glanced up at Austin, which was a mistake. He looked like he was on the verge of cracking up.

"Don't you dare," she mouthed silently.

The footsteps stopped nearby. How was she going to explain hiding behind an ice machine?

She bit down on a startled cry when the footsteps

came closer. She held her breath and closed her eyes, as if that would make her invisible.

She wanted to scream when the person's phone rang, and a guy whose voice she blessedly didn't recognize answered the call.

"Hey, yeah," he said. "Just got back to the hotel. Got the munchies so I'm standing here staring at a vending machine."

Ella didn't hear any sounds of coins clinking as they entered the payment slot or any chips or candy bars thunking into the tray at the bottom of the machine. No, instead she got to hear one side of a conversation that was growing more naughty by the second. Beyond frustrated, she allowed her head to fall forward onto Austin's chest.

When she felt a silent laugh shaking him, she gave his arm an equally silent swat.

"What are you wearing?" the guy asked whoever was on the other end of the call.

Had he honestly just asked that? She'd never had phone sex, but as she listened to the mystery man while pressed close to Austin's warm body, she began to understand the appeal. And from the way Austin's body was reacting, she wasn't the only one being affected.

When the guy asked his conversation partner to take everything off slowly and give him details, Ella wondered why he didn't just go to his room. But when Austin's lips captured the lobe of her ear, she forgot all about phone sex guy and focused entirely on the man with whom she'd been naked only minutes ago.

She barely contained a moan as his teeth replaced his lips and he tugged on her ear, then kissed the same spot. His hands slid up her sides until he was able to caress the sides of her breasts with his thumbs.

What was he trying to do, force her to reveal their hiding spot? She knew she should push away, stop this before it got out of hand, but she didn't. Everything he did to her felt too good to push away.

Wanting to show Austin that two could play this game, she reached around and grabbed his hips, pressing him closer to her. He growled, loud enough that she froze, afraid he'd given them away. But when she heard the other guy telling his partner to slip her hand into her underwear, she realized that he hadn't heard anything other than what the woman was whispering into his ear. Well, she had no idea if the other woman was whispering or not, but that's how she imagined it happening.

With agonizing slowness, Austin brought his hands to the sides of her face and lowered his mouth to hers. She opened for him, kissing him deeply, the conversation going on mere feet from them fading away as she pressed close to Austin. It was as if she were a sponge, soaking in everything about him—his warmth, his hardness, the texture of his tongue against hers, his male scent mingled with her own more feminine one. She was dying of thirst, and he was her endless supply of fresh, delicious water.

Somewhere at the back of her mind, she became aware of the little click of a key card activating a lock. She couldn't focus on the meaning with all her thoughts tied up in the sensations racing through her body. But then a door slammed across the hall, causing her to jump with a startled sound. She immediately covered her mouth with her hand, but she then realized that the man was no longer speaking.

Austin peeked around the edge of the ice machine. "He's gone."

Even knowing they were free to leave, Ella didn't move for several more seconds. Couldn't. Honestly, she was surprised her legs were still holding her upright.

Austin planted a gentle kiss on her forehead. "As much as I'd like to continue this, we better go before someone else comes in."

He wrapped his hand around hers and guided her toward the corridor once again. This time, no one was in sight. All Ella heard was the muted rumble of a man's voice in one of the rooms, and she wondered if phone sex guy had retreated to his bed to continue his hot-and-bothered conversation.

No, she couldn't think about that, or anything she and Austin had shared tonight, or she'd be dragging him back to his room with no regard for her dwindling chances of getting away unseen.

Though she still wasn't totally in the clear, she breathed easier once they were outside and walking down the sidewalk that led through the park. Even though they didn't speak, it didn't feel tense or awkward between them. She found that odd considering what had just happened. Of course, that might very well change in the morning, but for now it felt really nice to be walking through the night with him. When they reached her truck and she opened the door, he pushed her gently back against the edge of the seat and captured her mouth, kissing her as though he couldn't get enough of her. That was an intoxicating thought, one she understood fully because she could have easily stayed in that bed with Austin until he had to go back to Dallas. She promised herself that even if tonight was it, she wasn't going to regret one moment.

She resisted the completely wanton urge to pull him into the truck and make love to him again right there on Main Street. Damn, the man made her crazy.

Austin pulled away slightly but didn't release her. "See you in the morning?"

She nodded, not trusting her voice or what she might say.

He smiled. "Well, get going. Verona may have a network of nocturnal spies."

"I'd almost laugh at that as ridiculous, but it strangely wouldn't surprise me."

He gave her another quick kiss. "Be careful."

She relived her night with Austin on her drive home, remembering the slightly rough texture of his touch, the taste of strawberries mingling with that of all man, the very male scent of him that still accompanied her, clinging to her skin. She halfway hated to wash it away, but she headed for the shower when she walked into the house. She doubted she could sleep anymore tonight, so after the shower she went to work on finishing the tractor wheel table.

The sound of the night insects and the relative coolness of the air, the coolest it got during the summer in Texas, kept her company as she painted the stripped metal wheel and the metal legs a bright red.

While she waited for the paint to dry, she wandered through the piles of stuff she'd already brought home from the ranch and stored in the small shed. She ran her fingertips along the surface of the old sewing ma-

chine and got an idea. He'd told her about his grandfather's love of old John Wayne movies, a love they'd
shared. She could work with that.

Austin might say he wanted to keep nothing, but
she didn't believe it. She'd seen how he'd warmed
up to the ranch, slipping back into the person he'd
once been there, at least the part of him that had been
happy outside on the land. He still didn't come into
the house, but she wondered if she might be able to
change that with some time.

But she didn't have enough time. Unless...

The new idea that had sprung to life in her mind
continued to build through the rest of the night as she
stripped the old stain and touches of rust off the sewing machine. Excited about her idea to repurpose the
machine, she didn't want to leave the work in progress
when daylight started showing on the eastern horizon. But she still had lots to do at the ranch, even if
Austin agreed with what she was going to propose.

She stopped by the bakery for breakfast, and thankfully Keri wasn't working. This morning the early shift
was being handled by her sister-in-law Josephina. So
Ella was able to get out with her apple Danish and large
coffee without the inevitable questions that would no
doubt be making the rounds around town.

When she reached the ranch, she was surprised to
see Austin already there up on a ladder painting the
side of the house. An intense flutter of nervousness
filled her stomach, and she gripped the steering wheel
tighter. Yeah, facing him in the light of day was going
to be so awkward, especially after she'd climbed atop
him and had her way. Her face grew hot. Where had
she gotten the nerve to do that?

After parking and turning off the truck, she sat for a few moments, trying to bring her nerves under control. When she finally stepped out of the truck, she smiled as if they hadn't been naked and sliding against each other only hours before.

"You're tempting fate with that ladder," she called out.

"I don't know. Feeling pretty lucky this morning."

The wicked smile he gave her had absolutely nothing to do with ladders or paint. It made her want him all over again.

Attempting to not look like she was retreating inside, that's exactly what she did. Instead of working, however, she sank onto one of the kitchen chairs and started flipping through the family photos she'd been stacking there over the past several days while she ate her breakfast, drank her coffee and rehearsed what she wanted to say to him. Once she had finished eating, she took a deep breath and walked back outside. She nearly collided with Austin as she stepped out the front door.

"Good morning," he said, then pulled her into his arms and kissed her.

She didn't even attempt to resist and kissed him back. But somewhere in the midst of the mush he was making of her brain, she remembered why she'd come outside.

"I'd like to talk to you about something."

She saw the barrier go up in his expression. "That doesn't sound good."

"No, it's not bad. And it has nothing to do with last night."

Or did it?

She mentally shook her head. "I have an idea I'd like to float. I know you're set on selling this place, but I wondered if you'd perhaps consider renting it instead, to me. I need more space, and I think it's obvious I need more time to get through everything.

Austin removed his hat and ran his hand back through his hair. "I don't know."

"I wouldn't expect any sort of special treatment. I'd pay a fair rent if I can afford what you settle on."

He took a few steps away and looked down the driveway. "I hadn't planned on keeping an obligation here."

Pain jabbed Ella in the chest. She knew he wasn't talking about her, at least not specifically, but it hurt nonetheless. He'd said he wanted the ranch out of his life, but she'd thought she'd witnessed his attitude changing over the past several days. Maybe she'd seen only what she wanted to.

This had nothing to do with how she felt about Austin, though. Even if she never saw him again, she loved the idea of possibly renting this place. The view alone was more inspiring than her current one of the industrial park. Plus the storage and work space would be like a decade of Christmases rolled into one gift.

"If you're worried about having to constantly fix things, I can manage that on my own."

He shifted his gaze to her. The look on his face was filled with conflict and indecision. "I'll think about it. That's all I can promise right now."

She nodded, not willing to speak past the lump forming in her throat. The feeling of losing not only Austin but this place and all it could be to her and her business threatened to swamp Ella.

"I better get back to work," he said.

"Yeah, me, too." But as she watched him walk down the steps, all she wanted to do was cry.

AUSTIN WENT THROUGH the motions of painting the house, but his mind was definitely on the woman who was back to loading her truck as quickly as her legs would carry her. He could tell by her movements she was upset but trying not to show it. Trying, but failing.

Even knowing that, he couldn't just agree to her request. Keeping this place…he wasn't sure that a clean cut wasn't the best thing. If he still owned it, would it feel like he couldn't move on? That he'd be responsible for coming back here on occasion to check on things?

Would that be a bad thing? He'd lain awake a long time after walking Ella back to her truck following their amazing night together. He'd already been thinking about it happening again. But if he was going to break all ties, maybe it should just be one and done.

That sounded so cold, like she'd been nothing but a one-night stand. And that wasn't what she was, though he was having a difficult time finding the right description.

What he did know was that he hated that he'd upset her. And even if it would make leaving and severing all ties harder, he was going to put a smile back on her face.

When he finished painting the eastern side of the house, he climbed down the ladder and moved it to the back. Then he walked to the outside spigot and washed his hands. The next time she walked out of the house, he was standing at the top of the stairs holding one of the strawberry tarts he'd thankfully had enough sense to put in his hotel room's fridge the night before and kept chilled in a cooler since coming back to the ranch this morning.

"What's that for? It's not lunchtime."

"It's a peace offering."

"No need for that."

He pushed away from the porch support he'd been leaning against and moved closer to her. She held a crate of dishes from the kitchen like a protective barrier.

"I'm sorry I upset you earlier. You caught me by surprise, and it's a big decision. One I'd not even considered before."

"I understand you need to think about it. That's fine."

"Then why are you mad at me?"

She let out a slow breath. "I'm not. Just a lot on my mind."

He didn't think she was telling the truth, at least not the whole of it. But he let it go. All he wanted was to get back on her good side.

"How about I trade you? Delicious strawberry tart for that crate."

She hesitated, but her taste buds won out. "Don't drop it. I've got some great ideas for how to use those plates."

He looked down into the crate and recognized the white plates bordered by little blue flowers. "Gran got those at the grocery store, saved up stamps or something. I was so little I barely remember it. I do remember she brought them home one at a time."

The look on her face told him she was on the verge of asking if he wanted to keep the dishes.

"I don't need them. I get takeout a lot, so even the few dishes I have don't get used that often."

Though he didn't go into the house, he helped her finish loading her truck. When she turned around after shoving a final box in the bed of the truck, she bumped right into him. Austin took full advantage and wrapped his arms around her.

"We should go somewhere tonight we don't have to worry about anyone who knows us seeing and spreading gossip all over town."

She shook her head. "I don't have time. If I can't rent this place, I need every minute I can get to clear out everything here."

"What if I give you more time? I don't have to be here for you to be able to work."

"But you wanted to list the place before you left."

"I can postpone that a bit." One night with her and already he was changing his plans. That was either really good or really bad. He wasn't sure which.

"I don't know," she said, sounding conflicted.

Time for some persuading. He pulled her closer and lowered his mouth to hers, capturing it in a hungry kiss he'd been dying to give her all day.

"That is so much nicer than arm twisting," she said when they finally remembered to breathe.

Austin laughed. She made it so easy to do. If he wasn't careful, he was going to care for her too much.

Chapter Eleven

After how their first date had gone, Ella was surprised by how nervous she was as she waited for Austin to pick her up. She was actually ready early enough that she had plenty of time to pace the floor. If she didn't stop soon, she was either going to have blisters on her feet or wear a trench in the floor, or possibly both.

Why was she so anxious? They'd already shared more than most people going on only their second date. Maybe it was simply that it was the *second* date, more than she'd expected. She wouldn't have been surprised if their one smoking-hot night together had been it. A satisfying of their curiosity, a scratching of a persistent itch, nothing more.

But this second date—if she didn't know Austin would be leaving soon, it would be enough to raise her hopes that maybe they were heading toward an actual relationship. But he was leaving, and that meant she couldn't view Date No. 2 any differently than she had Date No. 1. Of course, now that made her wonder if it would end the same way—naked, sweaty and very, very satisfied.

When she heard a car slow on the road then turn into her driveway, she grabbed her purse and rushed out the front door before she could think about how that might look. She deliberately slowed her pace as she locked the door, then walked along the front walkway to where he'd parked.

Austin met her at the front of the car and stole a quick kiss that made her tingle all over.

"You look beautiful," he said, echoing his words from their first date.

And hearing those words was just as thrilling the second time.

Once they were in the car and he was backing out, she decided not to ask what his plans were for the evening. She'd liked the surprises their first date had offered so much that she was satisfied with going with the flow, seeing where the night took them. Knowing that her time with him was limited made her hyperaware that she needed to soak up every moment.

"You okay?" he asked as they turned onto the road that led east to Austin.

"Yeah, why?"

"You're quiet."

"Sorry. Thinking about work." Not in the slightest.

"Ouch."

She smiled. "Don't tell me I hurt your little ego."

He glanced over at her. "Someone's sassy."

She laughed and shifted her gaze to the surrounding landscape. The Hill Country had its own personality, with an interesting view in every direction. She loved it here, felt lucky that a chance day out with her friend Tamara had brought her to this place that almost immediately felt like home.

"Do you miss it here at all?" she asked.

"Honestly, I hadn't thought about it in a long time."

"And now?"

"I've enjoyed my time here more than I expected." He reached over and took her hand in his, making her wonder if he'd enjoyed it because of her but that it didn't change anything about his leaving.

She had to be realistic. No matter how drawn she felt to him, it wasn't reasonable to think he might change his entire life simply because they'd had some fun. No, best to focus on the moment and remind herself that becoming any more attached to him wasn't in her best interest. But she would have a good time tonight, no matter what.

For the next few minutes, they had a friendly argument over what to play on the radio. As many a disagreement had been settled over time, it came down to a game of rock, paper, scissors.

"Okay," she said, holding her fist against her palm as Austin held his against the steering wheel. "One, two, three."

A quick glance between them revealed her flattened-palm "paper" covered his fisted "rock."

"Ha! I win." She reached for the radio dial and turned it until she found some AC/DC, then proceeded to sing along.

"Just for this, you get to listen to all country on the way back."

She gave him an evil grin. "Who said I'm going back with you? I might get a better offer."

"Is that right?"

She laughed in response, pushing away the thought that she was going to miss this when he was gone.

When he suddenly pulled off the road and shoved the car into Park, she yelped.

"What are you doing?"

Austin took off his seat belt and leaned toward her, capturing her mouth with his own. The kiss set every nerve in her body ablaze. She shoved her fingers through his hair, drawing him even closer. It was like their kisses behind the ice machine times ten. Just when she thought she'd experienced the most awesome kiss imaginable, Austin upped his game and proved her wrong.

And then he pulled away, wearing a wide grin. "Still want a ride back with someone else?"

Ella knew she used to be able to speak, but the ability had evidently taken a hike as she stared at Austin and tried to recover from the earth-shattering kiss.

Austin chuckled and refastened his seat belt, then pulled back out onto the road.

"You seem very satisfied with yourself," she finally managed to say.

"Not bad, if I do say so myself." He glanced at her, still smiling. "You seem pretty satisfied with it, too."

Oh, she was far from satisfied. That would require more than kissing, and he probably knew it.

Left without a snappy response, she turned up the radio. Even the hard-rock guitars and lyrics couldn't drown out Austin's laughter.

As they got closer to the city, she had a hard time not thinking about how difficult it was going to be to go from steamy-hot kisses to, well, nothing. As she stared at the road in front of them, she wished she could be like a guy and not attach so much meaning to things that were just supposed to be casual and fun.

Don't think so much. Just be.

She spotted the line for the city limits and got an idea. "Pull over."

"What?"

She motioned toward the side of the road. "Pull over."

His naughty grin made her mind go to equally naughty places, but as soon as he parked she hopped out of the car.

"Um, where are you going?" Austin asked.

"Come on."

She caught the confused look on his face and giggled. *Take that, you big tease.*

When Austin shut off the engine and got out to join her, he scanned their surroundings. "You're not going to off me on the side of the road, are you?"

"Nah, you're evidently my ride home." She started walking up the side of the highway.

"What are you doing?"

She stopped and pointed toward the sign. "Getting your picture. After all, not everyone has a city named after them."

He ambled toward her. "Pretty sure the city was here long before me."

"Oh, details, details. Now go stand over there." She gestured toward the sign again.

"Women," he said, but there was no animosity or any real frustration in his tone.

When he reached the sign, he proceeded to hug it, one jean-clad leg lifted along the front.

"Goofball."

"Take it or leave it."

She'd take it, and wished she could take him, keep

him. Oh, jeez, there went her renewed determination to remain casual.

After a series of funny poses, she lowered her phone and propped one hand on her hip. "Come on, give me one decent shot."

At first she thought he'd refuse, but instead he leaned one forearm against the top of the sign and smiled at her. It wasn't one of those smiles meant to melt her insides, but it did nevertheless. Because this was the real Austin, the cowboy, even though he refused to acknowledge that's what he was at heart. Damn, she was going to miss that smile, the sound of his voice, the feel of him next to her.

"Okay, that's good." She turned and started retracing her steps to the car before she messed up and showed him how she felt about him. She wasn't willing to scare him off, not when she'd been looking forward to tonight ever since he'd convinced her to go out again.

"So, you going to make a big, blow-up poster of me?" Austin asked as he slipped back into the car beside her.

"Again with the thinking highly of yourself. Though I did hear they were in need of a new dartboard down at the Frothy Stein," she said, mentioning the bar that had been in Blue Falls longer than any of its residents.

Though she wanted to scroll through the photos she'd just taken, she slipped the phone back into her purse. Within a couple of minutes, Austin made a turn that would take them along a drive that afforded a lovely view of Lake Travis and the expensive homes dotting the area. When he pulled into the parking lot for Mizuumi, a high-end Japanese restaurant, her breath caught.

"I remembered you said you liked Japanese food," Austin said as he parked and switched off the engine.

Ella experienced the most ridiculous urge to cry, but she held it at bay. Her mouth already watered as culinary options raced through her mind.

When Austin took her hand as they walked inside, her heart filled with such an expansive warmth that she wanted nothing more than to be wrapped in his arms, just to be held by him as if he felt the same way about her.

How had she let herself get so close to him so quickly? Had she taken leave of her senses?

Her thoughts were interrupted by the maître d', who led them to a table next to the wall of windows that overlooked the lake. When he handed them their large, leather-bound menus, she had to fight the sensation that she didn't belong here. This was the type of place a man took a woman if he loved her, if he planned to propose. Neither of those things was true, so she forced herself to focus on the menu offerings.

"What are you having?" Austin asked.

"I don't know. Everything looks delicious."

"Yeah, it does."

The tone of his voice, deep and sexy as sin, caused her to look up. There was no doubt he wasn't talking about anything on the menu.

"Behave," she whispered.

He grinned. "That's no fun."

As she perused the menu, she started having fantasies about making sudden business trips to Dallas.

And if she just happened to bump into Austin, well, all the better.

The waiter arrived and thankfully pulled her back to the real world, one where she indulged in lobster stuffed with Dungeness crab and seafood risotto. She was going to make the most of this night in more ways than one.

Though she'd feared her blossoming feelings might cause her to be awkward in conversation, luckily their dining location for the evening offered a natural topic of conversation. She told him about some of her favorite memories of living in Japan, the foods she remembered eating, the older couple who had run a little market near where she'd lived who'd always given her panda cookies, the places she visited.

"What was your favorite?"

"There are so many, but something that really sticks out in my memory is the Tejikara Fire Festival." She could still remember the awe she'd felt watching the men carrying the portable shrines with millions of fire sparks shooting out of them. "It was like the Fourth of July times a thousand. Just beautiful."

When their food came, Ella was pretty sure she'd died and gone to taste bud heaven. And the fact that Austin seemed genuinely interested in all her tales of life in Japan and other duty stations just made the night even better.

After they finished their dessert of dango sweet dumplings, Ella was certain she'd never been happier in her life.

"Thanks for listening to me ramble on. I don't get to talk about my time in Japan much."

"Not even with your mom?"

She shook her head. "It makes her sad because we were all so happy then."

Austin reached across the table and took her hand in his. "You're the only person I've ever told about my grandparents."

Another piece of her heart opened up and let him in. She was allowing him to occupy too much real estate there, but she seemed helpless to stop it from happening.

"I'm glad you felt you could tell me."

He rubbed his thumb across the back of her hand, and she knew the teasing and lighthearted part of the evening was over. She also realized that she couldn't end this night the way she had after their first date. She had to stop her free fall before her heart went splat when he left to go back to his real life, leaving her to resume hers—alone.

AUSTIN SEARCHED BACK through what he'd said, trying to figure out what had changed so suddenly. He couldn't identify what it was, but it was as if the air around Ella had changed. It hadn't exactly chilled, more like it had ceased to move, as though she was holding it in check.

Maybe she was just tired. And if she was anything like him, she hadn't gotten much sleep lately.

He paid the bill, and at least Ella didn't pull away when he held her hand on their way out to the car. And when he brought her into the circle of his arms, she kissed him back with enough energy that he thought maybe he'd imagined the change in mood inside.

As they drove back toward Blue Falls, he didn't force conversation, instead holding her hand in his as he drove. The darkness of the night seemed to envelop them. He didn't even change the radio station as he'd threatened to do.

When he pulled into her driveway, he cut the engine and brought his lips to hers. He tasted the sugary sweetness of the dessert they'd shared.

"Come back with me," he said, aching for a repeat of their incredible night in bed.

When she hesitated, he knew for certain he hadn't imagined what he'd witnessed at the restaurant.

"Not tonight," she finally said.

"Is something wrong?"

"No," she said, squeezing his hand. "I had a wonderful evening. Thank you. I'm just… I think I'm hitting the wall and need a full night of uninterrupted sleep."

"Okay." Hell, no, it wasn't okay. At least not to his raging desire for her. But he wasn't going to be that guy who put his carnal needs before everything else. And maybe this was for the best.

Still, he kissed her for several minutes, and she let him. He almost asked her if she was sure about her earlier refusal, but he didn't. Instead, he caressed the side of her face.

"Go get some sleep."

She smiled, and it actually did look tired at the edges, as if she had a hard time mustering the energy to lift the appropriate muscles.

He sat with his headlights shining on her front walkway until she opened the door and slipped inside. Before he could follow her and beg to come inside, he put the car in Reverse. As he drove back to the

Wildflower Inn, he wondered how long it was going to take to get Ella out of his thoughts. If that was remotely possible. Or if he even wanted to.

Chapter Twelve

"This looks great."

As Paul Westberry, the customer who'd commissioned the tractor wheel table, ran his hand across the round glass top, a sense of pride swelled inside Ella. She was already riding high from how good her week was going—everything she'd been sharing with Austin, the fact that he was giving her more time to move items from the ranch and still considering if he might just rent the place to her instead of selling it, and now another happy customer.

"I'm glad you like it."

"You do good work. My dad is going to love this." He handed her the final payment for her work. "I'll be sure to recommend you to anyone looking for custom furniture."

"I appreciate it. Thank you."

She helped him load the table and watched as he left before going inside to get a glass of lemonade. It was hotter than Satan's underpants today. Before heading to the ranch, she was going to enjoy a leisurely drink while the cranking AC brought her body temperature down.

After plopping down in her favorite chair, she took

a long drink, then pressed the glass to her forehead. She'd been trying to keep busy so she wouldn't think about the fact that Austin was leaving today, and there was no telling when or if she'd ever see him again.

They'd had a nice time in Austin the night before, with some excellent kissing when he'd dropped her off. But she'd refused to sneak back into the inn again. True, she didn't want to be seen, but more than that she knew if she went to bed with him again, it was only going to compound the pain when he left today. Better to start pulling away and shielding herself as best she could.

Her stomach growled, so she went back to the kitchen and grabbed a can of mixed nuts to eat on the way to the ranch. She'd considered not going out there until Austin was already gone, but she thought that might telegraph her feelings too loudly.

The sound of knocking at her front door surprised her. She wasn't expecting any packages. Had Paul come back for some reason? Or maybe it was her landlord, though the rent wasn't due for another week and she always sent it on time even if she had to forgo some other things.

When she reached the door, however, Austin stood on the other side holding a big take-out bag from the Primrose Café and a bouquet of gorgeous bright flowers. Her heart leaped at the sight.

"What's all this?"

"A surprise," he said with a big smile that made her want to believe that today wasn't the end for them.

"You have remarkably good timing." She took a couple of steps back and opened the door wider. "Come on in."

Austin extended the bouquet to her, and she tried to remember the last time she'd been given flowers. Probably her senior prom.

"Thank you. They're beautiful." She brought the bouquet up to her nose and sniffed the flowers' lovely scent.

Austin stepped into the house and started to follow her to the kitchen. She was at the doorway between the rooms when she realized she didn't hear his steps anymore. She glanced back in time to see a tense, pale look on his face. But he wasn't looking at her. Instead, he was staring at where she'd been forced to store some of the items she'd brought back from the ranch, cramming them into the corners of her living room and the rest of the house until she determined if she'd be able to rent the ranch or need to seek out a large storage unit.

"It's not normally this full," she said.

It took what felt like forever for her words to penetrate whatever fog of claustrophobia he was in. She imagined the disgust he must be feeling, even though he almost hid it. Almost. Even though she knew his background, could understand why he had issues with crowded spaces, she couldn't deny that his reaction hurt. He knew that she wasn't like his grandparents. Or was he doubting that now?

She took a step toward him. "How about we eat outside?"

After what felt like the longest moment in the history of time, he shook his head. "No, I'm fine." He took a slow, deep breath, then gave her a smile she could tell was forced.

She almost insisted they go outside, but she stopped

herself. He was trying, and if this could help him get past…well, the past, then maybe she should urge him farther into the house instead of allowing him to retreat. Besides, this was who she was. Even if her home was more filled to the gills than usual, it wasn't as if she was ever going to not have supplies such as these on hand. Maybe not taking up space in her house if she could move to a bigger place, but somewhere on her property.

Looking more shaky than she'd ever seen him, Austin managed to put one foot in front of the other. She noticed that the cowboy boots were gone, replaced by the sneakers she'd seen him wearing when she met him. He was already leaving his rancher self behind and returning to the man who lived in Dallas.

But he was here, and with flowers and food. That had to mean something, right?

To his credit, he made it into the kitchen without passing out. He placed the bag of food on her little white distressed table.

"Whatever's in the bag smells good," she said, trying to get his mind off his surroundings.

"Uh, yeah. My stomach was growling all the way over here."

She smiled, and thank goodness he smiled back.

"What would you like to drink?"

"I want to say a beer, but probably not a good idea since I'm driving."

Driving back to Dallas. She really didn't want to think about that. "How about root beer instead?"

"Sounds good."

Ella opened the fridge to retrieve some cold drinks. "Where do you keep your plates?"

"Cabinet over the microwave."

She grabbed two root beer bottles and was in the process of standing back to her full height when she saw the cabinet Austin was about to open. The wrong one.

"No—"

But she was too late. She saw it happen in slow motion—Austin opening the cabinet, all the items she'd stuffed in there tumbling out as if attacking him, Austin jumping back.

"God, how do you live with this mess?"

The amount of revulsion in his voice hit her like a punch to the heart. This wasn't going to work.

Austin, evidently realizing what he'd said and the way in which he'd said it, looked up at her. She saw what looked like a war going on in his eyes before he shook his head.

"I can't do this."

He fled the kitchen, accidentally kicking an old metal flour sifter halfway across the room, and stalked back out the front door.

Was he leaving?

Trying and failing not to be hurt, she nevertheless followed him, fearing he'd somehow already be gone. But when she reached her small front porch, she saw that Austin had stopped at the bottom of the steps and was trying to get his breathing under control.

"I'm sorry," he said without turning to face her.

"I know." She did, even if it felt like every word, every look into his eyes was carving out another part of her heart.

He glanced back then, and a sheen of sweat was

visible on his forehead. "We could go down by the lake."

Ella didn't think she'd ever had such reversal of emotions so quickly in her life. Thrilled that he'd sought her out with lunch and flowers one minute and crushed the next, because no matter the reasoning it was obvious the way she was living disgusted him.

"I can't." She wasn't able to voice a reason, and by the look in Austin's eyes she could tell he knew why.

He continued to stare at her for a few more moments before giving what looked like a halfhearted nod. "Feel free to go to the ranch to work whenever you want. There's an extra key to the house in the tack room in the barn." He hesitated a moment more, as if searching for the right thing to say.

"Thanks. I appreciate it." She had to act as if everything was fine, as if her heart wasn't breaking, because she needed him to leave before she fell apart in front of him. "Well, you've got a long drive ahead of you, and I've got to go clean up the *mess* in my kitchen."

She hadn't meant to put the bitter edge on the word *mess* when she said it, but that's how it came out. And judging by how Austin winced, he'd heard it.

He opened his mouth as if to say something, but he seemed to rein in the words before they escaped. That or he'd had no idea what to say. She thought maybe that broke her heart even more.

"Bye, Ella." No, that's what broke her heart more.

"Bye." It came out a strangled whisper, but she couldn't have prevented that if she'd tried. Her whole body was beginning to shake, but somehow she kept it from showing.

Despite having said his farewell, Austin continued standing there staring at her for a few moments longer before he slowly turned and walked away.

As she watched Austin head toward his car, her heart broke more with each step. It was all she could do to hold back the need to beg him to stay. Instead, she let him go, telling herself it was for the best, for both of them.

But when Austin didn't even look at her as he drove away, she couldn't stop the tears. Despite every fiber of her common sense telling her not to, she'd still fallen in love with Austin and now had to figure out a way to fall back out.

AUSTIN FELT AS if he'd been awake for a week when he walked into his apartment and dropped his bag. The farther he'd driven away from Blue Falls, the more confused he'd become. Part of him wanted to turn around and apologize to Ella again, but the other part kept saying that it was good they'd parted when they had, how they had. That way they didn't get any more involved, and he was reminded that they were too different to be together.

Then why did he feel like someone had stomped his chest repeatedly?

Maybe a decent night of sleep in his own bed would help. As he walked across the hardwood floor toward the bedroom, his steps echoed. He stopped and looked around at the familiar surroundings, the simple, sparse furnishings. There was nothing here that he didn't use, that didn't serve a specific purpose. Just the way he liked it.

He walked into the bedroom and stripped down

to his underwear, wanting the empty bliss of sleep. He wouldn't have to think about the look on Ella's face when he'd left, how he hadn't allowed himself to look in her direction as he was driving away. He needed distance between them to clear his head, to remember that the life he had here in Dallas was what he wanted, that his time in Blue Falls had just been a temporary diversion resulting from the loss of his last family member.

Well, hell, thinking about his grandfather's passing sure didn't help him feel better.

He sank onto the side of the bed and braced his forearms on his legs. The silence surrounding him wasn't comforting, wasn't even true silence, not like what existed on the ranch. Of course, neither was totally quiet, but the quality of the distant sounds was a world apart. Traffic and the occasional car alarm versus the call of birds, the song of cicadas on the night air, the lowing of the cattle.

He shook his head. Wallowing in nostalgia wasn't going to help him readjust to real life.

Austin crawled into bed, but within five minutes he was so annoyed that he couldn't get comfortable and relax that he got up again and paced the apartment. Instead of finding comfort in its simplicity and order, however, it felt cold and impersonal. How was that possible when everything here belonged to him, had been chosen by him?

He knew why. Ella wasn't here. In such a short time, he'd grown used to her laughter, her smile, her teasing, how she could get excited about the design possibilities of everything from an old colander to a forgotten metal can. She was just one of those people it was pleasant to be around. She embraced life and all its chaos while he tried to keep life as neat and tidy as a spreadsheet.

"Damn it." How had he let his claustrophobia gain so much control over him?

He tried to convince himself that even if he didn't have a problem with crowded spaces, he and Ella would never work out. They were too different. Their lives were traveling different paths. She wanted to put down roots in the place he'd left behind so long ago, and Lealand Energy Group wasn't going to suddenly relocate its headquarters to a small town in the Hill Country. Too many obstacles any way he looked at it.

Then why couldn't he stop thinking about her and the fact that he'd started missing her the moment he left her standing alone in front of her house?

ELLA STEPPED BACK and admired her work. She realized it was possible that Austin might never see it, but she'd already been partially finished with it when he'd rushed out of her life. They didn't have a future, but something inside her wanted him to see that what she did mattered, had value. It wasn't to get him back in her life. That horse had left the barn. It was more standing up for what she believed in—herself and the quality of her work.

Keri stepped forward and ran her hand across the top of the desk. "This is beautiful." She turned to look at Ella. "Are you okay?"

"Yeah, why?" She hadn't told anyone about what had happened between her and Austin—the good or the bad.

Keri gave her a sympathetic smile. "You and

Austin—there was something there. I wasn't the only one who noticed it."

Ella sighed. "Doesn't matter now."

Keri stepped forward and gripped Ella's hands. "You can talk to me. Trust me when I say that keeping things bottled up inside isn't good for you. They tend to fester."

Ella dropped her gaze for a moment, then paced across the living room that was now empty except for the desk. Not having a use for it, she'd given the couch to a family in need that morning.

"I let a handsome face and my hormones overrule my common sense, all the while knowing it wouldn't amount to anything lasting."

"But you wanted it to."

Ella didn't know what to make of the fact that Keri's words were a statement instead of a question. Had she been that obvious about the feelings she was developing toward Austin?

"Yeah. I know that doesn't make sense."

"Why not? I think whoever said our feelings had to make sense was crazy. I mean, I never thought I'd fall in love with Simon. We'd been friends in high school, but then I spent years mad at him. Then everything changed, and now I can't imagine life without him. Don't want to."

"But he lived here. And I doubt he walked into your bakery and curled up his nose like he'd just arrived at the city dump."

Keri looked satisfyingly appalled. "Austin did that? What happened?"

Ella couldn't hold everything in anymore, and the

next thing she knew she was spilling the whole story, each word more difficult to say than the previous.

"I'm so sorry," Keri said when Ella was finished.

Ella shrugged, trying not to cry. "I just have to move on. I do hope that maybe I can rent this place. It's perfect for what I need."

"Is that wise, renting from him?"

"I figure I won't have to see or even talk to him. I'll send him a check once a month, and if there are any problems with the house I'll either take care of it myself or send him an email." She could be an adult about this. It wasn't as if she'd been married to the guy.

Keri looked doubtful about the wisdom of the idea, but Ella was of the "don't throw out the baby with the bathwater" mind-set. If she couldn't be with Austin, if he couldn't view what she did in the light she'd love for him to, then at least if she could make a positive step in her business it wouldn't all have been for naught.

Her heart ached at her pragmatic view, but she'd decided to try to focus on the positive rather than how much she could be angry or hurt if she allowed those feelings to overwhelm her.

Keri placed her finger atop the desk. "So, this?"

In the immediate aftermath of Austin's abrupt departure a week ago, she'd considered stripping what she'd done so far and starting over, making it something totally different she could sell. But despite everything, that hadn't felt right.

"I'd already started on it, a thank-you for allowing me to take all the stuff from here for free and giving me some business advice. How we parted didn't negate that."

"You're a good woman."

"I try." Though admittedly, sometimes it was hard. "Thanks for helping me carry the desk in."

"No problem. I gotta run, though. Have a wedding cake to make this afternoon."

A flash of Ella walking down the aisle toward Austin surprised her. She had to stop thinking that way. All it would do was prolong the ache in her chest, preventing her from moving on and recapturing the happy, positive person she normally was.

She walked out to the porch with Keri, then waved as her friend drove down the driveway toward the road. After taking a moment to soak up the peace and quiet, she went back inside for the last few items stored in the house.

Though it could benefit from some fresh coats of paint, the interior of the house looked so different from when she'd first stepped inside less than a month ago. She was trying not to get her hopes up too high, but she couldn't seem to prevent herself from imagining how she would personalize the space and make it her own. If her business really took off and she got more comfortable with her financial situation, maybe she'd just buy the property from Austin.

She shook her head, reminding herself to not let her fantasies get too carried away. With the future uncertain, she backed her truck up to the barn to finish filling up the empty space in the bed.

Ella stopped to scratch Duke on the nose. At least Austin had made arrangements with a neighbor to care for Duke and the cattle. She chuckled when Duke nuzzled the side of her face. Was he lonely out here, missing Austin? Maybe he still missed Mr. Bryant. She had no doubt that animals experienced loss the same as humans, so she took the time to talk to Duke while rubbing down his neck. If she was able to rent this place, maybe they could keep each other company and she could learn how to ride so she was comfortable doing it alone.

There she was, letting her imagination run away with itself again. But she couldn't help it. This place spoke to her, seemed to feed her soul and creative mind.

That thought was still bouncing around in her head when she headed out for the day. When she passed through the line of oak trees that hid the main part of the ranch from the road, she spotted a sign at the end of the driveway and hit the brakes.

Tears burned her eyes and turned the image of the for-sale real estate sign wavy. She supposed she had her answer about whether he would rent the ranch to her. Had he known that from the moment she'd asked him about it but led her to believe there was a chance?

Moments ago she'd been determined to move on, to not wallow in her hurt, but now anger welled up like a tidal wave approaching shore. Austin hadn't even had the decency to call her and tell her. Not even a text message. That she had to find out this way ticked her off. It took a lot to make her mad, but she'd officially just hit that point, so much so that she was tempted to drive over the top of the sign. The image of her tire tracks streaking across the big "For Sale" letters gave her a sense of satisfaction.

But she didn't do it. Instead, she blinked back the

hot tears trying to escape and pulled onto the road. As she made her way toward town, she came to the decision not to go back to the ranch. She had nowhere else to store what was left there. Austin would have to find someone else to haul it away, and she wasn't going to tell him that. Let him find out through the real estate agent or potential buyer.

Sure, she could rent storage, but she had plenty of materials to work with and had spent so much time loading, hauling and unloading lately that she hadn't had enough time to create and market. Well, that changed today.

If anyone asked her why she didn't finish clearing out the buildings, that's what she would tell them. What she wouldn't say was that she wasn't going back because being on the ranch where she'd shared her first kiss with Austin, where they had gotten to know each other during their picnic lunches, would finish breaking her heart.

ELLA COULDN'T QUIT COUGHING. Was she getting sick? Had she finally overextended herself physically and emotionally? Maybe her body was screaming, "Enough!" The coughing got worse as she came more fully awake.

Smoke! The cause of her breathing distress hit her with such force that she threw back her light quilt and leaped from the bed, only to be met with thicker smoke. She immediately dropped to her hands and knees. Panic slammed into her when she saw the orange glow of flames dancing in the living room. She was trapped. The fear threatened to strangle her more than the smoke. She had to get out.

She coughed again, hacking until her throat felt raw.

The window. Somehow she had the presence of mind to grab her purse, which contained her ID, money, truck keys and computer, from where it hung on the back of the desk chair, and crawled toward the window.

When she reached the wall and tried to open the window, it didn't budge. Panic exploded within her. She shoved up again, banging on the frame. "Come on, please!"

Finally, the window slid up so fast that she fell forward and banged her mouth against the bottom window rail. The coppery taste of blood mixed with the layer of ashy residue caused by the smoke.

Her mouth throbbing and her heart about to beat out of her chest, she crawled through the window and dropped down to the ground, scratching her exposed skin on the sad shrubbery lining the front of the house. She crawled away from the house and collapsed in the middle of the yard, sucking in great gulps of fresh air.

Though she was still coughing some and her throat was scratchy, she lifted herself to a sitting position and looked back toward her home. Through the open window she could see the flames, being fed by the rush of fresh oxygen. It looked like they'd made it to the bedroom. She was losing everything. Tears pooled in her eyes, but she blinked them back. Now she needed to get help. She reached into her purse for her phone, but the feel of the empty side pocket reminded her that the phone was in the charger on the kitchen counter. Already gone.

She glanced down the road toward the nearest

house, a quarter mile away. But as she dragged herself to her feet and headed toward the road, a vehicle slowed and pulled into the driveway.

"You okay?" a male voice called out.

She couldn't see more than a dark silhouette beyond his headlights, but he sounded like an older man.

"Call 911."

She knew it probably didn't take long, but it seemed like forever before the fire trucks showed up. Standing at the edge of the yard watching as the flames shot out the windows and licked up the side of the house, she'd never felt so helpless, so incredibly alone.

Everything she'd worked for, everything she'd built, gone in a matter of minutes. She thought of all those long hours she'd worked hauling things from the Bryant ranch, days in which she'd fallen for Austin. All of it had been for nothing. Now she was homeless, alone and brokenhearted, and she hated it with every cell in her body. This wasn't who she was, but right now it was hard to make lemonade out of life's lemons. The only thing she wanted was to curl up and cry until she couldn't cry anymore.

Tears streamed down her cheeks, and despite the fact that her yard was full of fire trucks and emergency personnel, she dropped to the ground and finally let the sobs break free.

AUSTIN SAT IN yet another meeting of department heads and had to concentrate much harder than normal to keep track of the conversation. His gaze kept drifting to the slice of blue sky he could see outside the conference room window.

"What are your thoughts, Austin?"

He jerked his attention back toward the head of the table, where Mr. Lealand was staring at him with an expectant and slightly annoyed expression on his face.

"I'm sorry," Austin said, even though a voice somewhere in his head was saying that no, he wasn't. In fact, he didn't give a hairy rat's ass about the items on today's agenda. That should shock him, but it didn't. But what was he going to do about it?

Until he figured that out, he fumbled his way through an answer that seemed to only halfway satisfy his boss. And again, he didn't care. He still hadn't let go of how ticked he'd been by Lealand's half-hearted condolences followed immediately by his sending Austin a to-do list that was filled with asinine, bullet-pointed tasks—things that could be done a better way if Lealand just kept to his lofty office and let the managers do the real work or things that didn't need attention at all.

"You okay?" his assistant, Miranda, asked softly as they left the meeting.

"Honestly, I don't know." She followed him into his office, where he went to stand beside the window. Thank God he wasn't still trapped in cubicle hell. Not being able to see outside had not played nicely with his claustrophobia.

"You've not been the same since you got back. Is there anything I can do?"

He leaned his hands against the window ledge. "No, this is something I have to figure out on my own." He looked over his shoulder. "But thank you."

She smiled then walked back out to her desk, leaving him alone. Miranda was good like that, being able to detect what he needed and when, reading his moods, saying the right thing at the right time. If only he had a fraction of her ability. He thought about asking her what to get for a woman when he wanted to apologize after really messing up, but then remembered that Ella wasn't the typical woman. She'd likely be happier with a truckload of old machinery parts than flowers and chocolates. Though she had appeared pleased by the bouquet he'd brought her that last day.

The sudden, powerful need to hear her voice hit him square in his chest. If nothing else, he needed to apologize for fleeing her house as if she were living in squalor.

He closed the door to his office and grabbed his cell off the edge of his desk. But when he called her number, it went to voice mail. Either she was busy or she was ignoring him. He could easily see the first and wouldn't blame her for the second. When the voice mail message started, he listened to her cheery message but hung up before the beep, not willing to say what he needed to say on a recording she might just erase without listening to it.

Since his workload wasn't getting any smaller with him just standing around, he forced himself to sit and start making some headway. He'd never had such a difficult time concentrating. Every time he started an email, he'd think about how nice it had been to get astride a horse again. While signing forms, he remembered the burn of muscles as he'd stripped the paint off the ranch house. As he ate take-out Chinese for lunch, he actually ached to be back on that patch-work quilt eating sandwiches with Ella.

He leaned back in his chair and ran a hand over

his face. When was he going to start feeling normal again?

The fortune cookie that had come with his black pepper chicken sat on his desk. He hated fortune cookies and normally just tossed them in the trash unopened. But since he wasn't really able to concentrate anyway, what the heck? He ripped open the plastic wrapper and cracked the cookie open. Who actually liked those things? He smoothed the crumbs off the little slip of paper and read the words it contained.

You cannot love your life until you live the life you love.

Even the fortune cookie knew what he'd been fighting ever since he'd come back to Dallas. This wasn't the place for him, not anymore. He couldn't believe such a brief return to his boyhood home had changed his outlook on what he wanted out of life so drastically. He'd thought he was happy here at Lealand, in his sparse apartment, with his casual relationships. But those days in Blue Falls, on the ranch, with Ella had shown him exactly how much was missing from his life.

But would she forgive him if she wouldn't even answer the phone when he called?

All he knew was that he had to tell her how he felt, that he cared for her. No, that wasn't quite right. He took a deep breath, then let it out slowly as he admitted to himself that he loved her. And if he had to beg her for a second chance, that's what he'd do.

Chapter Thirteen

Ella twirled her French fry through the blob of ketchup on her plate. Considering everything that had happened lately and how she'd missed several meals, she should be hungry. Only she wasn't. She ate because she had to, but she spent most of her time working with what few supplies were left to her. At least a dozen times a day she had to remind herself that things could be so much worse. She could have been seriously injured, burned, even died in the fire. The flames could have spread to the shed, consuming every last bit of her available materials, her ability to make a living.

It could have leaped to her truck and taken what had now become her temporary home. Turned out renting a new place was hard when you couldn't prove a steady income and your last home had burned down. She felt like taking out a full-page ad in the paper to announce the fire marshal's findings that the fire had been caused by faulty wiring, that it hadn't been deliberate or even negligent on her part.

No, it wasn't all bad. Her friends and neighbors had been kind, offering to let her stay in an extra room and organizing donations of clothing and other necessities. She knew she'd eventually land on her feet, but right now the ground and her nerves felt pretty shaky.

Unbidden, an image of Austin's strong arms holding her up formed in her mind. Sense memory had her remembering exactly how it felt to be held by those arms. Damn it, why couldn't she forget him?

"Feel like a piece of pie? The chocolate meringue looks really good."

Ella pulled herself up out of the quagmire of her thoughts and looked across the table at her mom. Around them, the locals and tourists filled the Primrose's every table. "No, thanks. But you have some."

"Maybe later. I think what I really need is to walk off what I just ate."

Ella glanced at her plate where two-thirds of her grilled ham and cheese and fries remained untouched. So different from how she'd devoured every morsel at Mizuumi, had soaked up every moment with Austin.

"A walk sounds good," she said as she stood so suddenly her chair almost tipped backward. She caught it in time and gave an apologetic smile to the woman at the next table who was sporting a T-shirt covered in bluebonnets.

Ella somehow managed to say the right things at the appropriate parts of the conversation as they walked down Main Street, stopping to window-shop in front of India Parrish's Yesterwear clothing boutique and going into Devon Newberry's A Good Yarn knitting shop to browse.

"I think I might try my hand at knitting," her mom said. "Maybe I'll get really good at it and open myself one of those little online stores."

It sounded too much like what her stepdad, Jerry,

would say about one of his new ventures, and it was the straw that broke Ella's emotional back.

"I'll be outside." Without waiting for a response, Ella retreated to the sidewalk.

But she didn't stop there. Though it was rude and inconsiderate, she kept walking. She couldn't stand still, couldn't utter one more word of meaningless small talk. What her mind and body cried out for was to run until her legs couldn't carry her one more step, scream until her voice failed her. But she did neither of those things. Instead, she walked toward the lake, all the way to the edge where the lapping water almost touched her toes. She watched a sailboat with a red-and-white-striped sail glide across the surface of the water, appearing as carefree as she wished she could feel.

Unable to hold in the latest batch of tears any longer, she sank onto a nearby bench and dropped her face into her hands and cried.

She recognized the approaching footsteps even before her mom sat beside her and wrapped her familiar arm around Ella's shoulders. Needing her mother's comfort, she let her mom pull her close.

"It's okay, sweetheart." Her mom rubbed up and down Ella's arm in a gesture Ella could remember from her earliest memories.

Her mom had done this same comforting ritual whenever Ella would grow scared of what might be under the bed or in her closet, or when she was sick, when nasty Teddy Lanham had picked on her in the third grade, when their next-door neighbor's teenage son had accidentally backed over Ella's bike the first day he had his driver's license. She only wished her current problems could be fixed as easily as nonexistent monsters or elementary school bullies.

"I know it's hard," her mom said. "But you're strong. You always have been. You'll get through this."

If it were only the fire, maybe, but it seemed as if everything had hit her all at once, crushing even her normal personality.

Ella sat up and wiped the remnants of her tears off her cheeks.

Her mom took Ella's hand between hers. "Come back to San Antonio with me. You can work from anywhere."

For a moment, Ella almost agreed. At least in San Antonio, she wouldn't see reminders of Austin everywhere she went. But she knew running wasn't the answer. She'd put too much into making a life here. Her rental house hadn't been her life. Her friends, this town, the business she was building were.

"I appreciate it, Mom, really I do, but this is my home now."

To her credit, her mom didn't argue with her, though Ella detected sadness in the way her mom looked out across the lake.

"You've always been so strong," her mom said. "Not like me."

"Mom—"

"No, it's true. I may be late to being independent, but I'm going to take inspiration from you, my strong girl."

Ella shifted on the bench to face her mom. Something was off, something that had nothing to do with Ella. "What do you mean?"

"I left Jerry."

"What?"

Her mom patted Ella's hand. "It's okay, really. It's been coming for a long time."

"I'm so sorry."

Her mom sighed but then gave Ella a shaky smile. "I'll be fine."

Ella leaned back against the bench. "Men suck."

"There it is, the real reason you're so upset. What's his name, and what did he do?" She sounded as if she might round up a posse and track him down for some Mom-style justice.

"You don't want to hear this."

"That's where you're wrong. I'm your mother. I'll always want to know what's going on with you, how I can help. I know we went through our difficult years, but you're the most important person in my life and I don't want to see you hurt."

She feared repeating the story of her brief but powerful relationship with Austin would make her heart finish shattering, but the words, like her tears, wouldn't be denied. Her mom listened without interrupting. When Ella finally shared the part about Austin's reaction to her home and how he'd fled, Ella had difficulty getting the words out past the lump in her throat. It felt as though she'd swallowed a lemon, and it had gotten stuck halfway down.

"I never fully understood what heartbreak felt like until that moment. I mean, of course I was heartbroken when Dad died, but—"

"It's a different kind of love, a different kind of heartbreak." Her mom knew it intimately, having lost the love of her life.

"I'm sorry. I didn't mean to bring up bad memories."

"Don't apologize. You've never talked to me about boys, and I know why. You were trying to protect me, even though I'd hurt you by marrying Jerry so quickly." She shook her head. "I knew from the beginning that it didn't feel right, but I think I was searching for anything that might take away the pain."

Ella understood that need now like she never could before. And yet… "I feel bad even comparing what you went through to what happened with Austin. You and Dad were together for years. I barely knew Austin."

Even speaking about him in the past tense hurt her heart.

"Sweetie, I knew the day I met your father that I was going to fall in love with him. Sometimes there is just a connection that is so powerful it cannot be denied."

That really wasn't what Ella needed to hear. What she wanted more than anything was to have her mom tell her that soon the pain would go away and she'd be able to return to her normal, happy self. That Austin would just be a memory of a few fun days.

"Maybe I should go back with you. We could get a place together."

Even before she finished speaking, her mother was shaking her head. "You thought you were just telling me about loving Austin—"

"I didn't say I loved him."

"Yes, you did. And it's obvious you love this town, the people here, the life you've built for yourself. It's a life worth fighting for, worth rebuilding. I'll help you any way I can, but I think it's time I finally stand on my own two feet, too."

They sat and talked for a long time, and Ella wondered if she and her mother had ever had such a lengthy, heart-to-heart conversation. Despite the fact her heart still felt banged up and bruised, she drew some comfort from a strengthening of her relationship with her mom.

When she walked her mom back to her car, a part of her wanted to beg her to stay, to not leave her alone. But she realized her mother was right—they both had to be strong and deal with their own problems, rebuild their own lives.

"You should try the knitting," Ella said. "There are tons of how-to videos online. I bet you'll be good at it."

Her mom reached up and cupped Ella's cheek. "My beautiful baby girl. If I find I have a hundredth of the talent you possess, I'll count myself a lucky woman."

Ella felt like crying again as she hugged her mom and watched her drive away down Main Street heading south. Not wanting to field questions about how she was doing from the well-meaning citizens of Blue Falls, Ella hurried to her truck and drove back out to where her house used to be.

She'd finished a project that morning when she couldn't sleep, so she went digging through the materials crammed into the little storage shed. But the inspiration that was usually there refused to make an appearance. Probably because every damn thing she picked up made her relive the look on Austin's face right before he'd run out of her life. With each item she picked up, be it a strip of lace or a piece of crockery, she grew a little angrier at Austin.

Angry at the way he'd left, angry that he'd made her fall for him, angry that he'd turned her life upside down. And most of all, angry that he'd broken her heart so completely.

Maybe the key to surviving and coming out the other side of this emotional funk was to focus on the anger and not the heartache. Anger wasn't normally part of her makeup either, but it was a hell of a lot better than feeling as if the sadness and loneliness were going to consume her heart.

THE FIRST THING Austin did after resigning from his position at Lealand Energy Group was call the real estate agent in Blue Falls and take the ranch off the market. He might end up failing at ranching in spectacular fashion, but he had to try. If he didn't, the what-if question would plague him the rest of his days. And if the ranching didn't work, he'd figure something else out. Because he wasn't giving up his family's home. As he headed back to Blue Falls, he couldn't believe how close he'd come to throwing away everything. He'd let the one bad thing blind him to all the good for too long. No longer.

As he drove up to the ranch, he half expected to see Ella's truck. But the driveway sat empty. His heart rate spiked as he walked up the front steps of the house and approached the front door. But the house would be cleared out by now, presenting no danger of him being buried by years of hoarding.

Though the house hadn't changed in size, the interior seemed enormous now that it was empty. Almost empty. He spotted what looked like his grandmother's old treadle sewing machine in the corner of the living room with a refinished ladder-back chair in front of it. But something looked different. He took a step he didn't think he'd ever take, and it echoed. He'd never heard an echo in this house.

When he reached the corner, his breath caught. Ella had converted the sewing machine into a desk with a glass top. Below the glass was a collage of the box covers from his grandfather's John Wayne movies—wearing an eye patch as Rooster Cogburn in *True Grit*, alongside Jimmy Stewart in *The Man Who Shot Liberty Valance*, as a coonskin cap–wearing Davy Crockett in *The Alamo*. She'd taken something he'd thought he never wanted to see again and proved him wrong.

As if that wasn't enough, she'd used an old window to frame photos from his youth. Him atop a horse he'd had as a kid, dressed from head to toe like a pint-size cowboy. One from when he was a toddler, chocolate frosting smeared from one ear to the other. His grandparents sitting on the front steps, smiling at the camera.

Austin swallowed against the raw emotion swelling in his throat at how much he missed them. He'd give anything to be able to go back in time and do things differently, not say things to hurt them, and take back how he'd told them they embarrassed him and he never wanted to live in their house again. He'd try harder to understand or at least accept the way they were. And he'd be kinder as he tried to make them understand his feelings.

He wandered into the kitchen, where only the big

appliances and the table and chairs remained. Atop the table were several photo albums and framed family snapshots Ella had obviously left for him despite his assertion he didn't want anything. He couldn't look at the photos now, wasn't ready to walk down that part of memory lane quite yet. Later, gradually.

A ticking sound drew his attention to the wall above the table. There hung one of his grandmother's blue floral plates, turned into a clock. He lifted his hand and ran his fingertip along the edge of the plate, remembering eating fried chicken and mashed potatoes off it. Ella really was good at her job, repurposing items in ways he could have never imagined. Giving items with old memories an avenue to create new memories.

And that she'd done it for him, after everything that had happened, said a lot about what a good person she was and meant more to him than he could find words to say.

He walked through the rest of the house, but when he went out to the barn to see Duke, who'd been left in the care of Jasper Clark, a rancher down the road, Austin was surprised to see that none of the accumulated items had been removed. A quick check of the other outbuildings revealed the same. Was Ella so angry at him that she'd decided even free materials weren't worth coming out here?

But that didn't make sense considering what she'd made for him, the care she'd taken in assembling all the family photos.

The need to see Ella, to apologize, propelled him back to his car. He had to make things right.

As he drove into downtown Blue Falls, he spotted the Mehlerhaus Bakery and got an idea. If he showed up with a strawberry tart as a peace offering, maybe she'd at least open the door and listen to what he had to say.

Keri looked up from where she was rolling dough on one of the big metal tables in the bakery's open kitchen. The fact that she froze and appeared surprised to see him tripped a warning alarm in his head. Had Ella told her what had happened? He hadn't considered that, since Ella had wanted to keep their time together quiet.

"Austin," Keri said as she approached the front counter. Yeah, definitely a chilly reception.

"I'd like to get a couple of your strawberry tarts."

"All sold out."

"Oh." He glanced at the glass-fronted display case, and didn't see any of the big cinnamon rolls Ella liked either. "What else does Ella like?"

When Keri didn't answer, he looked up to meet her gaze.

"Okay, I'm guessing she told you what happened, and I know I was a jerk. But I'm here to apologize," he said. "And I thought bearing something sweet might help me out a little."

"I don't think a pastry is going to help right now."

"I know I handled things badly. That's why I want to see her, to make amends."

Keri tilted her head a little. "You don't know, do you?"

Austin's gut wrenched. He didn't like the sound of that question. "What?"

"Ella's house burned down a few nights ago."

Fear slammed into him as if he'd been hit with the swing of a baseball bat. "Is she okay?"

"Some bumps and bruises, but she's lost almost everything."

"Where is she staying?"

Keri's expression tightened. "In her truck. She's trying to work using what little she has left in that shed that was behind the house."

He started for the door.

"Austin."

He stopped at the command in Keri's voice.

"Don't hurt her again," she said. "You do, and we're going to have a problem. Ella is one of the nicest people I've ever met. She doesn't deserve any of this."

He stared at Keri for a moment then nodded. "You're right."

Austin had a hard time not driving twice the speed limit on the way to Ella's place. When he made the turn onto the road that ran between the edge of the industrial park and her house, he felt sick. Only a charred shell of the house remained. The thought that she might have died in that fire scared him even though he knew she hadn't.

He closed the distance from the intersection to the driveway and pulled in. Her truck sat in front of the little shed, and she stood between them painting a chair. Though he wanted to race to her and pull her into his arms, reassuring himself that she was okay, he wasn't sure of his reception. So he slipped out of the car and walked toward her. He knew this wasn't going to be easy when she didn't even look up at him or acknowledge his presence.

"I'm glad you're okay," he said, at a loss for how to open the conversation, if she would even talk to him.

"Me, too."

Her response was cool, as if it was the first time she'd ever met him. No, even at their first meeting, she'd been bright and cheery, full of life. He hated that he saw none of that part of her personality now.

"Keri told me about the fire. I'm really sorry."

She looked up at him then, and the hardness of her gaze told him he'd hurt her more than he could have ever expected.

"Are you? I figured you'd think it was good that all of that junk was gone."

She might as well have slapped him. How was he even supposed to respond to that?

"Why are you even here?" she asked.

"I came back to apologize. I tried to call but couldn't reach you."

"Probably because my phone burned up."

Hell, this was not going well at all.

He took a couple of steps closer to her. In response, she stood up straighter and crossed her arms.

"All I'm asking is that you listen to what I have to say. Then if you don't want to see me again, I'll leave. I won't like it, but I will."

She didn't immediately respond but then said, "Fine."

"I am sorry, really sorry, for how I reacted that last day I was here, for what I said. I know you're not like my grandparents were, you actually use the things you accumulate, but in that moment… Well, it wasn't my finest."

He took another cautious step forward, and she didn't budge from her spot.

"I haven't stopped thinking about you since I left."

"About how you can't believe you were involved with me at all?"

"Ella, please don't. If I could go back and do things differently, I would. I promise you that. I've had a lot of time to think, and I know I have to let go of what happened in the past for good, to not let it have power over me at all. Trust me when I say I hate it and how I let it allow me to hurt you."

"Good. I hope you have a happier life now."

She said the words, but he couldn't tell if she meant them. Maybe she did, but the hurt was still coloring her tone.

"That's what I hope, too. It's why I came back here."

She tilted her head so slightly he almost didn't notice, but it was enough of a show of curiosity for him to push forward.

"When I got home, from the moment I walked into my apartment it didn't feel right. And when I went to work, all I could think about was being on the ranch, riding out amongst the herd, having the sun baking my back." He paused for a moment and waited until she met his gaze. "I missed our picnic lunches, the way you teased me about getting beaned in the head by the gutter, how much you love strawberry tarts and giant cinnamon rolls." He hazarded another step toward her, then two. "I missed you, Ella."

"We knew it was temporary. Our lives are in different places. We want different things out of life."

"That's what I'm trying to tell you. We don't."

She shifted her weight from one foot to the other. "What do you mean?"

"I quit my job. I'm going to make a go of running the ranch. And I want you there with me. There's plenty of room for you to work and store your supplies."

Ella held up a hand. "Wait. You're not making any sense. You don't even like what I do."

"You're wrong. I stopped by the house. I saw what you made for me. The desk, the picture frame, the clock, they're all beautiful." Another couple of steps forward. "You're beautiful, Ella. And I want to do whatever I can to make up for how I treated you that day I left, to make you happy."

She shook her head, looking confused or maybe as if she wasn't really hearing what she thought she was. "Why?"

He closed the distance between them and took hope from the fact that she didn't back away.

"Because I love you."

Her eyes widened so much he had the ridiculous urge to laugh but knew he couldn't.

"You…?"

He smiled. "You heard me right. I love you."

"How?"

At that, he did laugh. He couldn't help it. "How could I not?"

She shook her head again. "You're talking crazy. We had a bit of fun, but that was it."

"Is that really how you feel?"

She opened her mouth, but nothing came out. Something in her eyes told him that he wasn't the only one who had stronger feelings here.

"I thought it was just a little fun, too, but when you

weren't there anymore, I realized I'd fallen for you. Fast and hard, though I tried to tell myself it wasn't possible." He reached up and caressed her cheek with his thumb. "You're fun, hardworking, kind, so damn beautiful I don't understand why some man with eyes hasn't snapped you up. And did I mention great in bed?" He gave her a little, wicked grin, then grew serious. "And you made me realize I've been running from what I really want for a long time, ever since I left Blue Falls after high school."

Ella lowered her gaze and was quiet for so long that Austin thought she might not say anything in response. Maybe his love wasn't reciprocated. What the hell was he going to do then? Blue Falls wasn't so big that he'd never see her unless he became a hermit out on his ranch.

"You hurt me."

Her words, barely above a whisper, sucker punched him. "I know. I'm sorry."

"I...I thought I was the only one who felt something more, but I told myself that I wouldn't admit it because I knew you weren't staying. You were just passing through my life like so many other people have. Like everything I make. Nothing and no one stays for long. Saying that you meant more would just open me up to more hurt when you left." She paused. "But damn it, I fell for you anyway."

Austin's heart skipped a beat, then decided to beat faster. Was she saying she loved him, too? He couldn't believe how much he wanted to hear the words.

"When I saw the look of disgust on your face that day, it broke my heart because I knew I'd never see you again. That you didn't feel the same way I did, could never love someone who did the one thing you couldn't stand."

Austin placed his hand under her chin and gently lifted it so he could look into her dark eyes. "I want nothing more than the opportunity to heal the heart I broke. I promise you that you will never see that look on my face again. I can't say the claustrophobia has magically gone away, because it hasn't, but I will work my hardest to not let it have a hold over me anymore."

"You're telling the truth, about how you feel?" The hope shining bright in her eyes touched him.

"Every word. I love you, Ella Garcia, every curly-haired, pastry-loving, upcycling part of you."

For the first time since he'd arrived, he saw the beginnings of a smile. He pulled her into his arms and pressed his lips to hers. He felt like a man who'd been out to sea for months and had finally come back to shore and the woman he loved. He ran his fingers through her hair to the back of her head and deepened the kiss, unable to get enough of her.

After who knew how long, Ella pulled back enough to look up and meet his gaze.

"I love you, too. It scares me to say that, but I don't think I can keep it inside anymore."

He wound one of her curls around his finger. "Will you come live with me at the ranch? We can work together, on my work and yours."

"You'd do that, help with my business?"

"Yes. I mean, you've already helped me with fencing."

"Which you repaid by helping me with the business plan."

He tugged on her curl the slightest bit. "Our lives

aren't a balance sheet of favors. I will do whatever I can because I want you to be happy, and I know making your business successful will make you happy."

She looked up at him like she thought she might be dreaming. "You know what would make me happy right now?"

"A strawberry tart? Sorry, Keri's out. I checked."

She smiled and ran her hand up his chest slowly. "That wasn't what I had in mind."

Austin's lower half liked where her mind was heading. "Not to bring up bad memories, but we don't have a bed handy."

This time, she was the one to wear a wicked grin. "Pretty sure that car of yours has a backseat."

His pulse surged at the image that formed in his mind. "Does that mean I'm forgiven?"

"It's a good first step."

As he allowed her to lead him to the car, he couldn't agree more.

Epilogue

Ella couldn't sleep, not even with how wonderful it felt to be snuggled up next to Austin. Curiosity about what he'd been up to in the barn lately wouldn't let her mind rest. He'd said he'd reveal all on her birthday. Well, it'd been her birthday for about six hours now, and she couldn't wait a minute more.

She rolled over and started nibbling on Austin's ear. "Time to wake up," she whispered.

He groaned without opening his eyes. "You better be willing to make good on that promise."

She smiled. "You said you had a surprise for me today."

In the next moment, Austin rolled atop her. The feel of all that warm, taut, male flesh against her own skin scrambled her thoughts.

"You said you'd show me the barn today."

He gave her the wicked smile she'd come to love then lowered his mouth to hers. As usual, the passage of time faded as she got lost in his kisses. He really was quite good at them, among other things.

Austin moved his lips to her ear, nibbling as she had moments ago. "The barn will still be there later."

She gasped as he slowly entered her. Oh, this would never get old.

"What barn?" she said, causing Austin to chuckle in that way he had that made her tingle all over.

As they made love, she didn't care if the barn and its mysteries got swallowed by a black hole.

BY THE TIME they finally left the bed, showered and dressed, Ella could barely be still. Now that she wasn't captured in the wonderful haze of lovemaking, she was back to being intensely curious about Austin's secret project. She felt like a kid hopped up on too much sugar on Christmas morning.

"Okay, let's go before you pop, birthday girl," Austin said as he took her hand and led her outside.

She noticed a long, rectangular piece of birthday wrapping paper over the door to the barn, a big pink bow attached at one end. As they got closer, she saw a small rope attached to the paper at the opposite end.

"What's that?"

"Pull the rope and find out." He let go of her hand and nudged her forward.

Giggling and giving her hands a few quick claps, she hurried toward the thin rope. Up close, she realized it was affixed to the entire edge of the paper, giving her a way to unwrap whatever was underneath without having to climb a ladder.

Not having any clue what to expect, she took hold of the rope and pulled it sideways as she walked the length of the birthday hat–decorated wrapping. Once the paper was hanging by only a lower corner, she stepped back so she could see what she'd uncovered. She gasped and raised her hands to cover her mouth.

Hanging there over the barn's entrance was a wooden sign with the words "Restoration Decoration— What Was Old Is New Again" painted on it in what looked like the same shade of paint Austin had used on the exterior of the house.

Ella stared at the words, trying to understand what they meant. Finally, she turned and looked back at Austin. He smiled and stepped forward to take her hand again. Before she could form a question, he led her inside. At the sight in front of her, her heart swelled and her eyes blurred.

"Oh, Austin, it's too much."

He squeezed her hand. "No, it's not. You deserve this."

Ella let her eyes roam over the showroom he'd constructed of what looked like the front half of the barn. Rustic white walls surrounded her, and some of the upcycled lighting fixtures she'd made out of everything from teacups to old coffee cans to vintage silverware hung from the lowered ceiling. Several of her furniture pieces sat around the space, smaller items sitting atop them.

"How did you do all this without me hearing or seeing?"

"I have my ways. Remember, I'm a master at logistics. Plus, you're not always here." He smiled, and she hoped that smile was always a part of her life.

Realization hit her, the timing of her mother's most recent visit. "Mom was in on this."

"Yep. And so was Verona, Keri, Simon and his brothers. Pretty much half the town."

Her love for this man, her mom, her adopted home-

town, her friends and neighbors filled her with so much joy she thought she would surely burst.

Ella reached up and placed her hand on Austin's cheek. "Thank you. It's beautiful."

"It will be once you work your magic."

"Magic, huh?" She smiled. "We've come a long way from *junk*."

Austin pulled her into his arms. "Let's pretend I never used that word, okay?"

"Only if you kiss me."

"No hardship there." Austin lowered his mouth to hers and kissed her with the same passion he'd shown that first day in the rain, when she'd been faced with a big decision—run to protect herself from possible heartache or take a chance. She couldn't begin to express how thankful she was that she'd shoved caution away and told him she was interested in more.

Austin's lips left hers. "Come on."

"What? This isn't it?"

"You'll see." He slid his hand down her arm to claim her hand, then led her toward a door in the back of the newly enclosed space.

Beyond it lay a quarter of the barn he'd converted into a work space for her. Tools were arranged on hooks, in drawers and along the surface of a long workbench. And on the wall, he'd painted "One man's trash is another woman's treasure."

She smiled. "I like the change you made to the quote."

"It seemed appropriate."

"I love it all." She let her gaze roam over every little detail. "It's a dream come true."

She noticed another door in the side of the room. "Tell me you left poor Duke some space."

"Yeah, he and all my tack and equipment fit fine in what's left."

Ella opened the door and poked her head through. Duke raised his head at the sound and looked toward her.

"Hey, boy. How you like your new digs?"

Duke sneezed, making her laugh.

Austin came up behind her and spun her slowly to face him. "One more surprise."

"Austin, no. This is so much already."

"I took a page from your book and fixed up an old piece of furniture." He pointed toward an old wardrobe in the corner of the workshop.

He'd painted it red then obviously sanded it to give it the distressed look she liked. Her heart filled almost to bursting that he would have done this, so different from the man she'd met who thought her love of old things really odd.

"It's pretty."

"Go take a look. I made some shelves to hold supplies."

She stood on her tiptoes and kissed him on the cheek. "This is the best birthday ever. Only way it could be better is if you told me that my birthday cake isn't fattening. I am getting birthday cake, right?"

He chuckled and kissed her on the forehead. "Yes, ma'am, there will be cake later. Now go check out my handiwork."

She crossed to the wardrobe, then ran her hand along the surface of the doors. She smiled back over her shoulder. "Not bad for your first upcycling project."

Ella opened the two doors and saw he had indeed filled the wardrobe with shelves that would come in handy. Then her gaze found what looked like a small box. She moved closer and reached for it. The moment her fingers wrapped around it, her heartbeat skyrocketed. Could it be? Or was it, was all of this, a big, beautiful dream?

Her hands shook as she pulled the little black box from the wardrobe and opened it. She couldn't help the squeak of surprise she made when she saw the contents, a gorgeous diamond ring sitting in the midst of black velvet.

Slowly she turned and met Austin's eyes. "Am I dreaming?"

Austin took his time as he walked toward her, holding her gaze, causing her heart to beat more rapidly with each of his steps. When he reached her, he slipped the ring from the box and went down on one knee as though she was living in a fairy-tale romance.

As he looked up at her and she saw the depth of feeling in his beautiful blue eyes, she knew she'd never loved anyone so much in her entire life.

"I didn't expect you to come into my life, but I couldn't be happier you did. Not only did you make me see what I really wanted from my life, but you've shown me what true love feels like. And I never want to lose that feeling. So, Ella Garcia, will you please marry me?"

Tears welled in Ella's eyes. "You're sure?"

He smiled. "I wouldn't be down here if I wasn't."

She laughed, then nodded. "Yes. So much yes."

He slipped the ring onto her finger, and to continue her magical birthday, it fit perfectly.

She noticed the way the ring made her hand look different. "You shouldn't have spent money on something so expensive, not after everything else you've done for me."

Austin stood and held her hand in his, her palm down so the ring was on full display.

"Sometimes a woman deserves something that is just hers and hers alone."

Despite her love of making sure nothing was wasted, she couldn't deny she liked the idea that this ring would be special only to her and Austin, a symbol of how they felt for each other.

"I love you," she said, her voice thick with emotion.

Austin caressed her cheek with his thumb and raised her left hand to his lips. "And I love you."

Ella knew she would never tire of those words. A lifetime of hearing them seemed pretty good to her.

Perfect.

* * * * *

MILLS & BOON®

Desire™

PASSIONATE AND DRAMATIC LOVE STORIES

A sneak peek at next month's titles...

In stores from 10th March 2016:

- **Take Me, Cowboy** – Maisey Yates *and*
  His Baby Agenda – Katherine Garbera

- **A Surprise for the Sheikh** – Sarah M. Anderson *and*
  Reunited with the Rebel Billionaire – Catherine Mann

- **A Bargain with the Boss** – Barbara Dunlop *and*
  Secret Child, Royal Scandal – Cat Schield

Available at WHSmith, Tesco, Asda, Eason, Amazon and Apple

Just can't wait?
Buy our books online a month before they hit the shops!
visit www.millsandboon.co.uk

These books are also available in eBook format!

MILLS & BOON®

Helen Bianchin v Regency Collection!

0316_MB520

MILLS & BOON®

Why not subscribe?

Never miss a title and save money too!

Here's what's available to you if you join the exclusive **Mills & Boon® Book Club** today:

✦ *Titles up to a month ahead of the shops*
✦ *Amazing discounts*
✦ *Free P&P*
✦ *Earn Bonus Book points that can be redeemed against other titles and gifts*
✦ *Choose from monthly or pre-paid plans*

Still want more?
Well, if you join today, we'll even give you
50% OFF your first parcel!

So visit **www.millsandboon.co.uk/subs**
to be a part of this exclusive Book Club!